The building hoves into view and – by the cringe! There are half a dozen naked bods playing croquet on the lawn. I glance towards a peeling signboard poking out of the shrubbery and suddenly it comes to me – like the squitters after eating a couple of pounds of unripe apples. 'Little Crumbling Naturists' Sanctuary' – naturists not naturalists! The place is a nudist colony not a bird sanctuary.

'Oh fantastic!' I say. 'You're not barmy after all.'

Sylvia looks at me, puzzled. 'What do you mean?' she says.

'You're a nudist,' I say.

'Of course I am,' she says. 'So are you – aren't you?'

Also by Timothy Lea

Timothy Lea

Confessions from a Nudist Colony

Futura Publications Limited
A Futura Book

A Futura Book

First published in Great Britain in 1976
by Futura Publications Limited

ISBN 0 8600 7359 9

Printed in Great Britain by
Hazell Watson & Viney Ltd
Aylesbury, Bucks

Futura Publications Limited
110 Warner Road
Camberwell, London SE5

CONTENTS

Chapter Eight

In which Timmy is forced to go to unusual lengths in order to find a suitable candidate for The Miss Nude World contest.

Chapter Nine

In which Timmy gets to grips with the press in order to save The Wonderful World of Nudism.

Chapter Ten

In which Timmy and Sid move on and there is a more or less happy ending.

CHAPTER ONE

In which Timmy and Sid have a revealing brush with the fuzz on Clapham Common.

'Wonderful, isn't it?' says Sid. We have just come out of the Highwayman and he is gazing across the rolling expanse of couples trying to have it off in the middle of Clapham Common.

'The first bit of sun always brings them out,' I say.

'What are you on about?' says Sid irritably. 'I was referring to spring unfurling her mantle of green, not that bloke tucking his shirt down the front of that bird's skirt. I don't know how they have the gaul to carry on like that in front of everyone. That geezer with the brown demob suit and a pork pie hat ought to get amongst them with his sharpened stick.'

'The game warden?' I say. 'He's too busy stopping people stoning the crocuses. Anyway, what's got into you, Sid? They used to have to send a bloke round after you with a bucket of sand to fill in the dents. You're the last person to start casting asparagus.'

But Sid is not listening to me. He is still under the spell of spring and four pints of mild and bitter. 'Just grab a niff of that breeze,' he drools. 'You'd never think that had to blow over Clapham Junction to get here, would you?'

'To say nothing of ducking round Battersea Power Station,' I agree with him. 'Yes, Sid, it's a rare treat for the hooter, even after what you've just done.'

Sid takes a few brisk steps towards the pond where the middle-aged wankers crash their model boats into each other, and throws his arms wide. 'Not just the hooter,' he says. 'All the senses rejoice. Look at the little buds on that chestnut tree. Each one glistening under its coating of sooty smog. That's nature in blooming riot. Will our children ever see anything like this? That's what I ask myself.'

'I hope not,' I say, ripping my eyes away from the bloke who is clearly connected by more than mental ties to his lady love. 'They don't care, some of them, do they?'

'All over the grass,' says Sid in disgust. 'I don't know how they can bring themselves to do it. You'd think they'd just want to lie back and clock nature weaving her magic spell, wouldn't you?'

'Surely that's what gets them going,' I say. 'I mean look at that pigeon up there. He's not playing leapfrog with the other one. That's nature saying "get at it!"'

'Pigeons are always like that,' says Sid distastefully. 'You remember what they did to the seat of my bike? I only left it outside Reg Perkin's loft for a couple of minutes, too.'

'Yes, very embarrassing,' I say. 'Incidentally, the loose cover has just come back from the cleaners. I think Mum was hoping you might cough up a bit towards the bill.'

'What about my trousers?' says Sid. 'It's not my fault Reg Perkins can't house-train his bleeding pigeons. She ought to get on to him about it!'

'Just a thought, Sid,' I say, deciding quickly that there is little chance of making headway in that direction. 'Certainly is a lovely day.'

'Definitely!' Sid takes a deep breath and winces. 'When it's like this you couldn't consider living anywhere else, could you?'

'Er – yes,' I say. Sid's words sound a bit strange coming from a bloke who was quite happy bumming round the Mediterannean on SS *Tern* until an American admiral tried to run him down with his ship – he was unhappy because he had just seen Sid boarding another vessel with his

8

wife and a couple of camels. (See *Confessions from a Luxury Liner* for surprising details.)

'Finest country in the world,' waxes Sid. 'Don't ever let anyone else tell you different. We may have our problems but when the sun is shining – shit! Can't people control their animals? Bleeding notices everywhere and nobody takes a dicky bird. The only way they'd do any good is if you put them low enough to scrape your foot on. I'd like to see some geezer's horrible hound doing his business on the public thoroughfare. I'd follow him home and drop one in his front garden.'

'Highly sophisticated, Sid,' I venture. 'I hate to think what kind of aggro that could spark off. What do you fancy doing now? We could mosey down and collect our sausage.' (Sausage roll: dole = National Assistance).

'Nah,' says Sid, finishing scraping his shoe and dropping the stick into the bin reserved for icecream wrappers. 'It's always a bit crowded after the boozers have shut. Let's leave it to thin out. I hate to look as if I need the money.'

'You just take it to save hurting anyone's feelings, don't you, Sid?'

'And to keep it in the country,' says Sid. 'I reckon it's the least I can do. All those Micks and Pakis would have it back to BanglaDesh in no time – or any other part of Ireland you care to mention. That brings back memories, doesn't it?'

'You mean the couple having it off under the caravan?' I say.

'Nah,' says Sid. 'Don't you ever think about anything else? I was referring to the fair. I remember coming up here as a kid. I never had money to spend on anything but I used to watch the roundabouts whipping round and listen to the records. I thought it was great. It was better than the telly in those days.'

'There wasn't any telly in those days, was there?' I say.

'I thought you had to listen to the radio with a pair of ear-phones.'

'You've no sense of neuralgia, have you?' says Sid. 'I suppose you're too young. It's when you start slowing up a bit that you begin to remember.'

'Blimey!' I say. 'If you can hang on a minute, I'll nip into one of these caravans and see if anyone's got a violin. What's come over you? Nature, childhood. I've never known you like this.'

'It's a kind of menopause,' says Sid '– or I suppose you should say manopause. A time of life when you take stock of where you are and where you're going. Have you noticed anything unusual about me lately?'

'You fastened your cardigan to one of your fly buttons on Tuesday,' I say, trying to remember. 'Or was it Wednesday?'

'I don't mean that!' snaps Sid. 'I haven't had an idea what we're going to do next, have I? Normally, new career opportunities are bombarding my nut like flies round a steaming horse turd. But at the moment – nothing. I'm worried, I don't mind admitting it.'

'You mustn't get yourself in a state,' I comfort. 'Maybe we should venture beyond those screens at the Labour more often. They might have something right up our street.'

'I don't want to work on my own doorstep,' says Sid. 'Swanning round the Med gave me a taste for the wide open spaces. That's why I'm so contented up here. Look at the light on the sail of that yacht. The sun gives it an almost translucent quality – like when you're sitting on your mum's karsi.'

I take it that Sid is referring to the way the sun shines through the cracks in the door and focuses on the cut up bits of the TV Times in the bog paper holder but I don't really like to ask. 'I could certainly do with some bread,' I say.

'What for?' says Sid. 'What good's bread?'

His words strike me round the face with the force of an ice-cold halibut freshly wrenched from the Arctic Ocean.

'What good is bread?' I repeat. 'Everything we've ever done has been based on your desire to stash away a few bob.'

'I was young then,' says Sid. 'No more than a gullible boy with distorted values. I used to think that if money couldn't buy happiness at least you could live miserably in comfort, but I don't believe that any more. Look at Paul Getty.'

'That's not him, is it?' I say. 'Behind the thermos with the blonde bird? She's a bit young for him, isn't—?'

'No!' says Sid, cuttingly. 'I meant examine the situation of Paul Getty and ask yourself if he has found true happiness. I've realised that money isn't the answer, Timmo. There's much more to life than sipping your Bovril out of a gold-plated mug in front of "Match of the Day" in colour.'

'And you don't think Paul Getty has realised that?'

'I *do* think he's realised that,' says Sid emphatically. 'But he's realised it too late. That's why he's always looking so blooming miserable. I don't intend to make the same mistake.'

'Thank gawd!' I say. 'You'd have been unbearable as the richest man in the world.'

Sid ignores what some might have considered to be a trace of sarcasm in my voice. 'The only thing, is that having rejected riches, I don't know where to turn. I'm in a state of limbo. Timbo – I mean, Timmo.'

'Well,' I say. 'As it so happens, fate has directed us to the right spot. Look what it says on that caravan. "Madame

Necroma reveals all: £1". Your future laid bare for a couple of bars, Sid. Can't be bad.'

I am not really serious but Sid's mince pies light up. 'Yeah!' he says. 'She should know, shouldn't she? They have a gift these people. Lend us a quid.'

'Do me a favour!' I say. 'She can make do with the gifts she's already got. I've already bought most of the booze you drunk in that rubber. Anyway, I'm very happy with you in a state of limbo. It doesn't cost me money.'

'There you go again,' says Sid. 'Money. It's your BO and end all, isn't it? You can't think about anything else. You're so inflexible. If it wasn't for my ability to mellow and develop as a human being you'd be exactly where you were when I first met you.'

'Don't make it sound too tempting,' I say.

'What I always have difficulty in making you understand,' says Sid, 'is that you have a wonderful opportunity to learn from my experience in life. I go through things so that you don't have to.'

'Like my fiancée,' I say.

'You're not still worrying about that,' says Sid. 'It was so long ago – and anyway, you were never properly engaged.'

'Wouldn't have made any difference if we'd been getting married,' I say wearily. 'You'd have been trying to feel her up while you handed me the ring.'

'No need to be coarse,' says Sid. 'That's all behind us now – all that sexual foolishness. Now I'm a more mature human being I can see what Mary Whitehouse and Lord Longford are up to.'

'You've heard rumours, have you?' I say, beginning to get interested. 'Don't tell me that nice Antonia Fraser's daddy has done something untoward.'

'Of course not!' says Sid. 'I didn't mean "up to" in the slap and tickle sense. I was referring to their stand against the corrupting influence of books like the ones your dad keeps in the hallstand.'

'He doesn't any more,' I say. 'They're in the cistern.'

'Blimey, I wondered why he was in there for so long. Dirty old sod! How did you find out?'

'I pulled the chain one day and nothing happened—'

'You have to pull it quickly and then give it one long pull,' interrupts Sid.

'Do you mind?' I tell him. 'It is my home. I ought to know how to use the karsi. Why don't you belt up and let me finish?' I pause for a censorial moment – good word that, isn't it? – and then continue. 'When I climbed up on the seat I found that a couple of mags has slipped underneath the ballcock.'

'How very appropriate,' says Sid. 'They must have been a bit soggy.'

'They were,' I say. 'But it didn't spoil the effect. The photos on the reverse side of the page showed through so you had one bird on top of the other.'

'You had that anyway,' says Sid. 'Oh dear. How sad it all is. Your Dad has grown old without achieving maturity. I'd feel sorry for him if he wasn't such a miserable old git. Lend us a quid.'

I had hoped to talk Sid out of his insane impulse to help Madame Necroma towards a new set of frilly curtains for her caravan but once he gets an idea into his crust it can be very hard to budge. We are still arguing when one of the curtains is pulled aside and a bird with a beauty spot and a lot of makeup snatches a gander at us. She looks a bit ruffled, as does the geezer who appears when the caravan door opens. His knees are practically the first thing to hit the top step and he staggers down the rest of them like he has both feet through the slit of his y-fronts.

'Find it all right, did you?' asks Sid.

The bloke looks not a little taken aback. 'What do you mean?' he says suspiciously.

'You know,' says Sid, jerking his head towards the window. 'Does she know her stuff?'

The bloke gives a little shiver and pulls his mac around him. 'Unbelievable,' he says.

Sid turns to me. 'There you are! Come on, don't be a berk. Maybe she'll take something off for the two of us.'

'She won't take anything off,' says the bloke. 'I asked her specially.'

'Well, we'll have a go anyway,' says Sid. 'Come on, Timmo! Don't you want to know what the future holds in store?'

The bloke gives Sid another funny look and hurries away muttering. 'Nice chap,' says Sid. 'He clearly found it a moving experience. Did you notice that glazed look in his eyes?'

'I was concentrating on the way his knees bashed together,' I say. 'Do you really want to go through with this, Sid?'

'Definitely,' says my diabolical brother-in-law. And he bounds up the steps like a jack rabbit.

No sooner is his Oliver Twist poised in front of the Rory than it whips open and the bird in the window nearly clocks him one with one of her enormous earrings. They are so big that you could sit a parrot on them – provided you did not mind running the risk of it doing its business in your earhole. She is now wearing a head scarf tied tightly round her nut and her generous knockers heave beneath an embroidered shawl.

'Madame Necroma?' says Sid. 'Good afternoon, madame. My friend and I would like to avail ourselves of your service.'

'Both of you?' says the bird.

'Exactly,' says Sid. 'You have perceived my meaning to

14

the T. We were wondering if there was a possibility of you making a reduction in our case?'

'I'll reduce anything you show me,' says Madame Necroma. 'Come in boys. You don't want to hang about. There's narks everywhere. It's getting impossible to turn over a couple of bob without finding a copper.'

She closes the door behind us and we take a gander round the inside of the caravan. 'Blimey,' says Sid. 'I never seen one with a double bed in it before.'

'It folds away to make a couple of work surfaces,' says Madame. 'Now, what can I do to accommodate you? Both together? Or, one at a time? Or one watching? – it's amazing how popular watching has become lately. I suppose it's the telly?'

'What's the cheapest?' I ask quickly.

'One at a time, flat rate,' says Madame. 'A quid each.'

'You go ahead,' I say to Sid. 'I'll give it a miss. I'm not all that keen.'

'Charming!' says Madame Necroma.

'Don't take it to heart,' says Sid. 'It's a question of bees, not doubting your professional integrity. We're both the same sign anyway. Scorpio: brooding, sensual, possessive—'

'Skint!' says Madame Necroma.

'I'll wait for you outside,' I say to Sid.

'Right,' says Sid. 'Don't fret. Whatever I learn will be to our mutual advantage. This might be the turning point, Timmo. It could be the best quid you've ever spent.'

I am still trying to tell him that I only lent him the money when Madame Necroma pushes me down the steps. She certainly seems in a hurry to get on with it. I suppose Sid's stars could be on the point of moving into a different quarter. I believe it is a very precise science.

When I get outside I have a quick shufti round the fair

and then take a butchers at the couples on the common. I soon give this up because the other people who are clocking them are such a disgusting lot. It's like pornography. There is nothing wrong with it except the kind of person it attracts. It makes you feel dirty to be associated with them.

About ten minutes have gone by and I reckon that Madame Necroma must have finished with Sid. She did not look the type to hang about. I wander back to the caravan and am slightly surprised that there is no sign of Clapham's answer to Paul Newman. Nor is there any sound from the caravan. Madame must still be gazing intently into her crystal ball. Best to leave them at it rather than interrupt the seance, or whatever it is. Sid would be furious if I spoilt his big moment.

I have just started counting the china alsatians in the caravan windows when I turn and see a female copper surveying me with what would pass for interest in any other bird. I don't know what it is but I immediately start feeling guilty. My palms get hot and sweaty and when I move it is as if I expected a jemmy to drop out of my trouser leg. I turn away but I am conscious that the bird is still watching me. Perhaps she thinks I am casing the caravans prior to a spot of B. and E.

'Psssst!' Do my senses deceive me or is it her making that noise? I turn and she waggles a finger at me and retires behind a trailer. What can she want? Perhaps it is a new way of arresting people. You nip round the corner after PC Niceparts and a blooming great bule bashes you over the nut with his truncheon. Still, what have I got to worry about? I haven't done anything. I take a deep breath and trip round the side of the trailer – some twit has left an electric cable stretched across the grass. The Bluebird is waiting for me and, I must say, she could take me in charge any day of the week. Neat as a guardsman's sewing kit and eyes like warm toffee. She has a delicate dust of freckles on her face and her eyelashes flop about like they have just been washed and she can't do a thing with them. All in all, she looks as if she would find it difficult to straighten a seam in her stocking, let alone arrest anyone.

'CID?' she murmurs. She is nodding over my shoulder when she speaks and I am so busy clocking the plus features that for some reason I think she is referring to Sid – we often call him El Cid, anyway.

'Er-yes,' I say, not wanting to give too much away. You never know what Sid has been up to.

'Balham,' she breathes. 'Sorry I'm late for our Romeo Victor. Has there been much action?'

I don't answer at once because I am trying to work out who this Romeo Victor bloke is. Perhaps I misheard her and she said Romany Victor. That would make more sense in our present surroundings. 'Look,' I say. 'I think there's been a mistake.'

'You were expecting a man.' To my surprise her lip starts to tremble. It is a nice lip, as is its plump little friend underneath, and a wave of sympathy runs through my Y-fronts.

'Only Sid,' I say.

'I don't know Sid,' she says. 'I've only just joined the station.'

'Balham,' I say. 'Oh yes, you said.'

'I won't let you down,' says the bird. 'I may only be a woman but inside me beats the heart of a man.'

'Blimey!' I say. 'I bet that made the Police Gazette. It's wonderful what surgeons can do these days, isn't it?'

For a moment, I think the bird is going to burst into tears.

'You're making fun of me!' she accuses. 'I was referring to Elizabeth the First's words at Tilbury.'

'Oh, them,' I say. 'Yes, well, you should have made yourself clear. I missed that episode when it was on the telly. What precisely are you trying to say to me?'

'I'm trying to say that you can rely on me,' she says. 'I won't let you down. I don't care what they're doing in there. I won't be shocked. Just say the word and I'll be right with you – oh!' While I am wondering what the hell she is talking about she suddenly whips a pair of handcuffs from under her skirt and slaps them on my wrists. God knows where she keeps her truncheon.

'Don't look surprised!' she hisses. 'Somebody's watching us from the window. I'll pretend to arrest you.'

I glance up at the window of Madame Necroma's caravan and am not a little taken aback to see Sid blinking down at me. He looks strangely flushed and dishevelled. Maybe it is the surprise of seeing me being led off by one of the female fuzz. I raise my manacled mits along with my eyebrows and his boat race is joined by Madame Necroma's. She is looking a bit on the heated side and I can't help wondering what they have been doing. Surely it is beyond the realms of possibility that kapok karate has been indulged in? Before I can indulge the horrible thought to excess, the female copper has led me round the corner and is feeling in the pocket of her tunic.

'Sorry about that,' she says, sounding like Barbara Cartland watching one of her pekes relieve itself against your ankle. 'I thought they might think it was a bit fishy if they saw us hanging about outside the caravan – oh no!'

Her face goes all horror-struck like Harold Wilson looking at the latest trade figures and I am swift to realise that something is wrong. 'Look,' I say. 'I don't want to sound unsympathetic and I always used to enjoy Z cars, but what is going on around here?'

'I've lost the key to the handcuffs,' she says. 'Oh gosh. You're going to think I'm an awful goose.'

'At the very least,' I say. 'Look, you could get arrested for this. Everybody's looking at me.'

'Come over to the car,' she says. 'Perhaps the driver will have a spare one. I am most awfully sorry about this.'

'So you should be!' I hiss. Honestly, you feel like sticking your tongue out at Jack Warner, don't you? No wonder the country is in a mess. I wonder this kid was able to cut out the application form without doing herself a serious injury. She must have needed guidance to follow the dotted lines round the advertisement. If she was not easy on the eye-balls I might be thinking about writing to my MP.

'What's he done, Miss?' says one of the kids who is clustering around us.

'Child murder!' I tell him. 'Hop it you horrible little basket!'

'Looks a villain,' says another God forbid. 'Do you want any help, miss?'

'No thanks,' I say. 'I'm going quietly. Which is more than you will be if you don't scarper sharpish!' I make a threatening lunge and they drop back half a dozen paces.

There is a police car parked under a tree and the bloke at the wheel puts down his copy of *Six Hundred Ways To Thump Someone And Leave No Trace* and leaps out hungrily. 'Got the ponce, have you?' he says looking me up and down hungrily. 'Wait till we get you back to the station, matey.'

'No!' says little Miss Blue Serge, blushing. 'He's our contact. I locked him up by mistake.'

'Oh, gawd, Millie!' says the fuzz. 'I thought you'd finished for the day when you arrested that store detective for shop lifting. Unlock him quick!'

'I've lost my key,' says the bird. Her lip has started trembling again and it is clear that she is on the verge of tears.

'Oh no!' The rosser bashes his fist against the side of his nut so hard that his hat nearly falls off.

'Haven't you got one?' says Millie.

'Course I haven't got one!' The fuzz looks about him desperately. 'Who's keeping the caravan under surveillance?'

'Nobody,' says Millie. 'I'd better go—'

'No you don't! You've done enough damage for one day,' says the fuzz. 'You stay here. I'll go.'

'What about me?' I say.

'You can't go,' says the copper. 'Not with those handcuffs on. You get in the car with WPC Marjoribanks. I'll be back as soon as I can.'

'Thanks a lot,' I say, not without a trace of sarcasm.

'Sorry about this,' says the male fuzz, considerately opening the car door for me. 'These combined ops are always a bit of a disaster, aren't they? Get out of it!!' His last remark is delivered to the pack of kids round the car as he turns and strides purposefully towards the caravans. The kids follow him.

WPC Marjoribanks slides along the back seat beside me. She has nice little knees and I can't help clocking the curve of her thighs underneath the blue serge skirt. 'Alone at last,' I say.

She smiles nervously. 'I don't have to say it again, do I?'

'Please don't,' I say. 'It doesn't help very much. Haven't you got a hack saw tucked away somewhere?'

She does not answer but starts running her hands over the front of her body. 'I must have a hole,' she says.

'It's not beyond the realms of possibility,' I say suavely. 'Perhaps you'd better have a look for it. I shouldn't think anything would have much chance of dropping out of that lot.'

I am clocking the front of her tight tunic when I speak and it is true that she would be pushed to smuggle a thin stamp hinge in the space not taken up by knocker.

'I suppose there's always a chance,' she says.

The same thought occurs to me as I watch her fingers

delving in the breast pocket of her tunic and a wave of naughtiness sweeps over the maximum stress area of my jeans.

'Any luck?' I say.

'Oh dear,' she says. 'There is a hole. The lining's gone.'

Not surprising with that lot chafing against it, I think to myself. 'Perhaps its slipped down inside,' I say, jerking my manacled mits to indicate that some kind of action needs to be taken.

WPC Marjoribanks nods and starts to undo her tunic. She is wearing a plum red half cut bra under her blue shirt and I suck in my breath appreciatively. 'That's not government issue, is it?' I say.

'What, the shirt?' she says.

'The bra,' I say. 'I can't help noticing it when I look. It's nice.'

'Oh, no, it's not – I mean, it's not police issue. Frankly – if it doesn't sound like heresy – I'm not all that keen on the uniform. In fact—' her lips starts to tremble again '– I'm not all that keen on the Force.'

'I don't like force either,' I say. 'There's too much of it. People talk about sex and violence like they are the same thing but I only see the—'

'I mean the Police Force,' she says. 'Frankly I don't think I'm cut out to be a copper. That probably sounds terrible to you. How long have you been a flat foot?'

'Well, I've always had a bit of trouble with my arches,' I say. 'Mum made me wear my sister's old sandals when I was a kid and—'

'A policeman,' she says. 'How long have you been with the CID?'

This time I twig what she says: the CID not the SID. She has obviously mistaken me for a plain clothes copper. I wonder if it would be wise to disillusion her? Especially in our present situation. 'Not very long,' I say. I give a light laugh and wait for her to ask me why.

'What are you laughing at?' she says.

'I was just thinking,' I say. 'If I wanted to make a pass at you I'd have a problem, wouldn't I?' I hold out my wrists and give her the famous Lea slow burn. It is all good clean fun and she smiles gamely.

'I sometimes wonder if that's why I joined,' she says sadly.

'What do you mean?' I say.

'I used to be very free and easy,' she says. 'I remember how worried my mother was. I think I thought that if I joined the police force it would be the next best thing to becoming a nun. I'd be protected from myself. The sanctity of the uniform would keep me on the straight and narrow.'

You could nip on my straight and narrow any day of the week, I think to myself. I nod understandingly and take one of her hands in both of mine – I don't have any alternative with the handcuffs on. 'You don't want to go against your true nature,' I say. 'Any luck with that key?'

She retrieves her hand and runs it along the hem of her skirt. 'Nope. It must have dropped out.'

'Couldn't have slipped inside your shirt?' I drop my tethered mits on her Ned Kelly and have a little feel. It is even more sexy with the bracelets on. Percy certainly thinks so anyway. He bounces up like a rubber pigeon shit. 'No. There's nothing there – except you.' The minute I lay hands on her she stiffens like something else I have just mentioned and it is clear that the pressure of my sensitive looks and lingers is not altogether repugnant.

'This is awful,' she says. 'What would anyone say if they could see?'

'There's nobody around to see,' I say. 'They've all gone off with your mate. Let's make sure you're not concealing anything.'

I lower my nut in time with my voice and gently brush my mouth against hers. I wouldn't exactly say that she abandons herself to my lips but she does not bust the back window jerking her head away.

'Are you married?' she says. 'All the worst ones at the station are married.'

'I'm not surprised you have problems,' I say. 'No, I'm not married.'

'You shouldn't be doing that,' she says.

'I'm just trying to keep the circulation running through my wrists,' I say. 'These handcuffs are blooming tight.'

'Isn't there anything else you can feel?' she says.

'I don't know,' I say. 'I'll have to find out.' Before she can say anything, I drop my mits to her knee and twist my body round so that I can slide them underneath her skirt.

'Ooh!' she says.

'The steel's a bit cold, is it?' I say – consideration for birds' feelings has always been one of my strong points.

'Not only that,' she says. 'Your cheek's pretty cool too! I've never worked with any one like you.'

'We could become famous in the anals of crime,' I say.

'I think you mean annals,' she says. 'Though when you do that with your hands I'm not sure.'

'I'm sorry,' I say. 'These seats slope down a bit steep.' I give her another chance to taste the nectar of my lips and this time our cakeholes melt together and I feel her long lashes brushing against my cheek like imprisoned butter-flies – poetry, isn't it? Oh, all right, please yourself. Only trying to extend my range. And, talking about extensions – yes, Percy is rearing roofwards like he is bent on turning my lap into an imitation of a tent being erected. She has gorgeous lips, this bird. They are sort of soft and tacky so that they form themselves to the shape of your cakehole and then cling on like clams. What a bleeding shame that my mits are manacled. I really feel the urge to mould this

23

bird-sized bule to the stressed steel that is the Lea rib cage.

'Stop! You must—' she squawks.

'Careful,' I say. 'Anything you say will be taken down and used to wipe the condensation off the inside of the windows.' I have already managed to check that her grumble is no stranger to the velvet gong-belter and without further ado I give her knicks a sponsored trip to kneesville.

'Stop!' she squeaks. 'This is terribly naughty. Supposing we have to make a sprint for it?'

'Make a splint for it?' I say. 'There's no danger of that I can assure you. Clock this.'

'No!!' she squeals as I seize my opportunity to reveal Britain's latest space probe financed entirely by pubic subscriptions. 'I was referring to our raid on the vice ring. We may be called into action at any moment.' She gazes into my lap and I see her mind grappling with the problem of what use I can be with my hands manacled and an enormous hard on. I suppose I could always try to batter down the door of a caravan if the worst came to the worst.

'Get on my lap,' I say. 'Go on. You know you want to.' If she doesn't, I want it enough for both of us. By the cringe! You could paint my nob tartan and call it Throb Roy.

'Oh, you're terrible!' To my relief she bends forward and helps her knicks over her ankles. 'Are they all like you in the CID?'

'Yes,' I say. 'You want to ask for a transfer.' I raise my arms above my head and she takes a quick shufti out of the window and scrambles across my knees. They are steaming up fast – I mean, the windows not my knees – and it is probably just as well that a discreet veil should be drawn over the proceedings.

'I could be discharged for this,' she pants.

'Likewise,' I say working my khyber forward to the edge of the seat. 'Mind how you – ah!'

She tucks my hampton away like your mum bunging a pair of freshly washed socks into a bottom drawer and it is clear that she is no stranger to parking inside the car.

'I had a boyfriend with a midget,' she says.

'Oh, I'm sorry,' I say. 'Still, they say that size isn't everything.'

'An MG Midget,' she says. 'It was very cramped.'

'Of course,' I say, getting her drift. 'This is spacious, isn't it?' I slip my wrists over her head and shoulders and hug her to me so that the handcuffs press into the small of her back. Honestly, if you want to get into the police this is the only way. The experience could only be improved if she took her hat off but you don't like to say anything, do you? Not at a moment like this. It might spoil the magic.

'Ooooh!' she gasps. 'I never realised that pounding the beat could be such fun.'

'It's not bad, is it?' I say. 'Oooh!' One of the problems of not being able to use my hands is that I have no control over any of my safety valves. Millie the Fuzz is strictly in the driving seat and with her dishing out the pelvic aggro the time to blast off can be measured in seconds. I try to think of Ted Heath's organ to take my mind off what the copper bottom is doing to me but it is no good. Wisps of hair are hanging down in front of her boat race and she is biting her lip. I hate to see a woman doing a man's work so I tilt my head forward and bite her lip for her. Not only bite it but suck it and send my tongue in to check that there has been no serious damage. This clearly goes down a treat and Millie joggles around so much that she hops off my hampton. 'Damn!' Boy! If all escaped prisoners were recaptured so quickly you would never hear that they had got out in the first place. WPC Marjoribanks gets my dick back on duty in a vulgar fraction of a second and I drive my feet down against the floor of the car. God knows what is happening outside. All the windows are totally steamed up.

'Awwwwwweeeeee!!!!' Millie lets out a squeak and then cements herself to my cakehole. Her body has stopped juddering up and down but a long tremor ripples through it and her toes press against the carpet. I can feel myself teetering on the brink and I jerk my fife upwards until the chava lava runs wild through my quivering thighs and I feel like an electric blanket having it off with a cake mixer. It is a very affecting experience.

'Right, let's have you – blimey!!' The speaker is Millie's mate who has just wrenched open the back door. He looks harrassed and surprised, in that order. 'Millie! You're supposed to be on the job.'

'Would you like to rephrase that statement?' I say.

'It was bad enough with that bloke in the charge room,' says the male fuzz. 'You were only supposed to be taking him a cup of tea.'

'I was only trying to soften him up,' protests Millie. 'Why must you keep bringing up my past?'

'Time to move on is it, chief?' I say. 'Don't worry about leaving me. I'll be all right.' It has occurred to my shrewd brain that the sooner the two coppers slope off the better. What I had with Millie was very beautiful but it could not last. It was just a flash in the pants really. If I arrived home with a female fuzz Dad would have a heart attack – on second thoughts –

'You're a disgrace to the uniform,' says the male copper. 'Come Marjoribanks. Button your tunic and shove your knickers down the back of the seat with the rest of them. There's work to be done.' He turns back to me. 'You'd better wait here.'

26

'Have no fear, squire,' I tell him. 'I'm not going anywhere.'

I am blooming nearly right, too. Have you ever tried pulling up a pair of trousers with handcuffs on? – no! not on the trousers. Why would anyone want to handcuff a pair of trousers? Wake up! This isn't exactly highbrow reading but you are supposed to have a certain amount of nous. Now, where was I? Oh yes. Standing beside this police car with my bum hanging out of my jeans. I can't make any progress inside the vehicle and it is only when I straighten up that I begin to get somewhere – like nearly arrested again. I feel such a berk giving little jumps in the air and trying to pull my trousers up at the same moment. A couple of old ladies give me a very nasty look and though I can't lip read I reckon they are looking around for a keeper. Ungrateful old bags! You'd think they would be glad of a bit of excitement at their age, wouldn't you?

In the end I manage to tuck my fife away and I am ready to scarper. My shirt is hanging out at the back but I can't do anything about that with the handcuffs on and nobody is going to draw any conclusions. I mean, it is often like that when you come out of the karsi, isn't it?

I take a few steps along the road and then remember Sid. Is he still nattering to Madame Necroma or will he have come out and wondered where I am? I had better slip back and have a discreet decco. Millie and her mate seemed interested in the lady so I had better step warily.

I approach the fair from a different angle and carefully pick my way through the caravans. The fair is now in full swing and the music is grinding out above the hum of the generators. I come round a corner and focus on Madame Necroma's caravan just as the door opens and the good lady appears at the top of the steps. She is looking decidedly dishevelled and unhappy and pulling a coat round her shoulders. Behind her appears Millie looking embarrassed and I sink back into the shadows. The driver of the police car is the last to leave and he looks round behind him before closing the door. Where is Sid?

'You've got nothing on me!' says Madame Necroma. 'Bleeding fuzz! I'll have you for this.' She turns on Millie. 'You'll have the curse for seven years!'

Before I can work out quite what she means by this statement, the trio disappear round a caravan. How very strange. I can only imagine that Sid has emerged and sloped off to his pad in trendy Vauxhall. He was never the patient type. But hist, what ist? The caravan seems to be trembling. Maybe I had better take a butchers. I keep a tight grip on the front of my round the houses and shuffle across the bruised grass littered with fag packets. Up the steps and I try the door. It opens. Inside, it looks just as it did when I last saw it. There is a bowl of Japanese fighting fish but they can't be belting each other hard enough to set up the vibration that is running through the caravan. I look down at the crumpled bed and – wait a minute! There is only half a bed compared with what there used to be. I switch my gaze to the side of the caravan and see a piece of material I recognise. It is a fragment of Sid's lumber jacket – we call it that because it is so diabolical that nobody knows how he could have lumbered himself with it. It is protruding from the door of a cupboard. The door of a cupboard that is shuddering as if someone is pressing against it from the inside. Could it be that –? No! It seems impossible – but yet – stranger things have happened to Sidney Noggett.

I grab hold of the handle in the wall and pull. Nothing happens so I pull with both hands and my trousers fall down. Hardly have they touched the floor than the missing half of Madame Necroma's bed swings down to carpet level. On it sprawls the bright pink body of a naked man lying amongst a pile of discarded clothing and crumpled

28

Tarot cards. His face looks like a chimpanzee's bum after it has slid down a helter skelter without a mat.

'Blimey!' I say. 'Are you all right, Sid?'

Sid does not answer me but looks round the caravan. 'Don't say she's gone!' he says. 'We were just getting to the interesting part.'

CHAPTER TWO

In which Timmy and Sid venture to Little Crumbling and meet tempting Dimity Dropwort before immersing themselves in two interesting Romany ladies.

'I can't believe that she was a nail,' says Sid.

'Stands to reason,' I say. 'That's why the fuzz had the caravan under surveillance. I bet they're pumping her down at the station at this very minute.'

Sid winces and then shakes his hand sadly. 'I thought she had something,' he says.

'I wouldn't be surprised,' I say, 'You'd better have a dunk with the dettol. Use one of the egg cups if you can get your –'

'I didn't mean that!' says Sid. 'Where's your romantic streak? I was referring to our instantaneous report.'

'You mean rapport,' I say. 'A report is a bang – still, I suppose, when you come to think of it –'

'Sometimes you meet someone and it's as if you've known them all your life,' muses Sid. 'Making love seemed as natural as the couple of quid I gave her.'

'I thought you didn't have any money?' I say.

'I found I had another quid on me,' says Sid. 'I reckon it would have worked, too.'

'What would have worked?' I say.

'She said that she would be able to get nearer to the reality that was me if we made love.'

'And did she?' I ask.

'I don't know,' says Sid. 'There was this bang on the door and "wump!" She presses a button and half the bed with me on it whips into the wall.'

'So you got nothing out of her?' I say.

'I wouldn't say that,' says Sid. 'She was completely at one with me about the environment. She had this feeling that our heritage was very precious and that we would squander it at our peril.'

'That's nice,' I say.

'And she resolved my uncertainty about the future,' says Sid. 'With her help I think I've found the answer.' He leans back and taps his nail file against the end of his finger.

'Go on,' I say. I am referring to Sid's effort to cut through the handcuffs with Mum's nail file but he is making indifferent progress and is clearly more interested in his latest crack-pot scheme.

'You might well cock your lug holes,' he says. 'This little number represents everything I feel like doing at the moment. A return to nature and a life free from stress and strain. I can almost hear the rooks crowing.'

'Cocks crow,' I say. 'Rooks caw. What is it, Sid? Put me out of my misery.'

'A camping site by the seaside,' says Sid. 'What could be simpler?'

'You mean caravans?' I ask.

'Caravans, tents, anything. All you need is a bit of water and somewhere for them to have a Tom Tit and clean their Teds. A field will do. It's a doddle to look after, and all the time you've got the sky as a ceiling above your head. You wake to the sound of birdsong. You're in the middle of people who are enjoying themselves. And the moment was never riper. With this once great country of ours temporarily in diarrhoea straits, more and more families are taking holidays at home, discovering the joys of their own countryside.'

'Where are you thinking of doing this?' I ask.

Sid rubs his hands together. 'Funny you should say that. When it came to a site I really fell on my feet.'

'They look as if something fell on them,' I say – somebody once described Sid as comatose and hammer toes.

'Don't take the piss,' says Sid. 'You're going the right way to get a button down hooter when you go on like that. Just ask intelligent questions and you might learn something.'

'Which one of Madame Necroma's relations owns a field near the sea?' I ask.

'Her aunt,' says Sid. 'Wait a minute! How did you know she had a relation who owned a field?'

'I've got mystic powers,' I say. 'I can foretell every time you are going to be conned. How much did you pay for this place?'

'I haven't paid anything yet,' says Sid. 'I'm not a fool! I'm not going to buy it without seeing it. It might be totally unsuitable. Really, Timmo, you do get up my bracket when you imply that I'm some kind of Charlie when it comes to sussing out job opportunities.'

He is still fuming when Dad comes in. I am a bit choked because I had not wished to be caught in a situation which might alarm my sensitive parent. 'What have you two skiving 'arstards been doing?' he says as I thrust my arms out of sight beneath the table.

'Nothing,' I say automatically.

'I can believe that,' says Dad. 'Now, I'm going to say two words that should strike terror into your hearts: hard work.'

'Why? Do you want us to translate them for you?' says Sid.

Dad is clearly feeling righteous after putting in one of his irregular days at the lost property office and does not warm to Sid's merry quip. 'Bleeding disgrace!' he snarls. 'A working man does an honest day's labour and he has to put up with two of his family behaving like bloody kids.

Haven't you got anything better to do than hop about in sacks?'

'Ah – yes,' says Sid. 'Sacks. Well, we're trying to get fit, aren't we?'

In fact, what happened is a bit more complicated than that. The fuzz take most of Sid's clothes with them when they leave the caravan and when Madame Necroma's old man comes in and finds a naked Sid trying to pull up the trousers of a bloke wearing handcuffs he gets the wrong idea. You can't blame him really. I mean, we live in disturbing times when what went for our grandfathers does not even make us think about coming. When he throws us down the steps of the caravan we are in a bit of a quandary and it is just as well that there is this pile of sacks lying behind the coconut shy. We slip two on sharpish and hop off home. Probably the most knackering experience I have ever undergone, especially coming after Millie – not that I did come after Millie. I am pretty certain that we came at the same time. Anyway, it helped to disguise Sid's naughty parts and the fact that I was wearing handcuffs.

'I'll tell you how to get fit,' says Dad. 'Do some bleeding work! The country can't afford to support grasshoppers any more.'

'If it can support you, it can support anybody,' says Sid. 'Grasshoppers, arse hoppers, you name it!'

'Hello dear,' says Mum, coming in with a tray of tannic poisoning – or tea as she calls it. 'Did you get your certificate all right?'

'Oh!' says Sid. 'Been down to Doctor Khan, have we? How long did he give you this time?'

'He doesn't know what he's talking about!' says Dad. 'He's useless if you don't wear a turban.'

'Don't be like that,' says Sid. 'That curry powder did wonders with your warts.'

'And you know who owns the supermarket where I had

33

to buy it?' complains Dad. 'Only his blooming brother-in-law. I remember when you used to get your stuff at a chemist. He told Mrs Kedge to wear a lentil poultice and it was leaking out of her knickers all down the high street.'

'Walter!' Mum jerks up the spout of the tea pot in protest.

'Well it's true. It's no good trying to draw a veil over these things. It's like this business of having to pay for your medical certificate. It's profiteering off the sick and needy.'

'So you've been down the library all day?' accuses Sid. 'Queueing up with the dossers to have a crack at the page three nude in The Sun.'

'Some swine tore it out!' says Dad. 'That's nice, isn't it? Tax payers' money and all. I wouldn't be surprised if it was one of Khan's lot. They like white women.'

'Well, that's only fair,' says Sid. 'I mean, you like black women, don't you? I remember how choked you were when you thought those African birds were going to have to cover up their knockers on the telly.'

'Sidney!' says Mum.

'Nearly turned him against the monarchy, it did,' says Sid. 'He couldn't make up his mind whether to write to Buckingham Palace or Bernard Delfont. In the end he chose Bernard Delfont because he was more influential.'

'It was the artistic licence I was worried about,' says Dad.

'You ought to be more worried about the TV licence,' says Mum. 'We've had three reminders and you still haven't done anything.'

'What have you got there?' asks Dad. Like a berk, I have raised my hands to grab the tea and Dad has clocked my wrists.

'He's got his cufflinks tangled,' says Sid. 'Nice aren't they? A bit on the large side but handsome.'

34

'It's nothing to be alarmed about,' I say. 'This bird thought I was something else – I mean someone else.'

'Picked you out in an identity parade, did she?' says Dad. 'Don't worry, my son. They'll never make it stick. What did you do? Nick her handbag. Where is it?'

'I didn't nick anything,' I say.

'You don't have to lie to me, son,' says Dad. 'I'm your father. I'll stick by you. We may have our ups and downs but when the chips are down we Leas stick together.'

'Look –' says Sid.

'Shut up!' says Dad. 'You led him into this, I suppose? Made him the catspaw for your evil designs. Played on his simple nature.'

'What do you mean simple?' I say.

'Your father's right, dear,' says Mum. 'Don't let them put words into your mouth. Say you never touched the girl.'

'I didn't touch the girl,' I say. 'I mean, not like that I didn't.'

'Of course, it could go badly with him,' says Dad. 'There's his criminal record to be taken into consideration.'

'Don't be daft!' I say. 'The only criminal record I've got is The Laughing Policeman.'

'He laughs in the teeth of danger!' says Sid. 'Makes you proud, doesn't it? Shall I start piling the furniture against the door? How long do you think we'll be able to hold out? Better nip out and get a few cans of beans before they get round here.'

'Shut up, Sid!' I say. 'You're not funny. Haven't we got anything stronger than this nail file, Dad?'

'Of course!' says he from whose loins I sprung with understandable haste. 'Is that the best he could do for you my son? Hang on a minute, I'll get my blow torch.'

'I'll go quietly!' I scream, leaping to the window.

'Now see what you've done,' says Sid. 'You've inflamed

his persecution mania. Why don't you calm down and start baking him a cake with a file in it?'

'Because, if his mother made it he'd never be able to bite through to the file,' says Dad.

'Walter!' Mum is understandably upset. 'How could you? Haven't I made a nice home for you and the kiddies? Why do you have to say a thing like that? If you don't like my cooking, you know what you can do.'

'Yeah. Go on gobbling down the bicarbonate of soda like I do at the moment. Don't make a scene for Gawd's sake. There's more important things to worry about.'

At this moment, fraught with unpleasantness and overhung by a thin veil of menace, the doorbell rings.

'Who's that?' says Mum.

Sid takes a decco through the lace curtain. 'Blimey!' he says. 'It's the fuzz!'

'Don't take the piss,' I say, 'Let me have a – oh no!' Standing on the doorstep and tucking thoughtfully at his helmet strap is an enormous copper.

'Right!' says Dad. 'I'll handle this. You get out the back and pretend you're pushing the lawnmower down to the shelter. I don't want the neighbours to notice anything.'

'They'll notice you haven't got a lawn,' says Sid.

'Shut up!' says Dad.

'Dad,' I say. 'I don't think—'

'I know you don't,' says Dad .'That's why I have to do it for you. Now, get out there and stop arguing.'

'Your father knows best,' says Mum. 'Stay in the shed till we come for you. Check there's nobody round the back, Sid.' When they go on like that you really feel that you have done something and I begin to wonder if my spot of in and out with Millie was against the law in more senses than one.

'Right,' says Dad. 'Here we go.'

'Don't antagonise them, Walter,' calls Mum.

'You can rely on me,' says Dad.

'There's nobody round the back,' says Sid. 'Come on, Bogart!' He pushes me out of the back door as I hear Dad opening the front.

The lawmower Dad was talking about is another piece he has 'saved' from the lost property office where he is supposed to work. The only piece of grass in the back yard it growing between its rusty blades and the roller stops going round after two yards. I abandon it, not caring whether the neighbours are watching or not, and go and sit in the corrugated iron shelter which Dad kept from the last war and which now holds most of his world famous collection of gas masks. There is a large wooden wireless with a lot of fretwork on the front of it, a tattered copy of a magazine called 'John Bull' and a Players fag packet with a bearded matelot as part of the design. This is where Dad must have repulsed Hitler. I wonder how he is doing with the fuzz? I am reading about how some geezer called Alvar Liddell planned his rock garden when Sid sticks his head round the door.

'Well,' he says. 'They've gone.'

'Oh good,' I say. 'Mum and Dad all right?'

'It's them that's gone!' says Sid. 'Blimey, your old man didn't half ask for it. The copper had only come round to tell him that the reflector on his bike had dropped out. Your Dad had his helmet off seconds after he opened the door. Screaming about a police state at the top of his voice, he was. Then your Mum waded in. She's strong, isn't she?'

'When she gets worked up,' I say. 'Oh my Gawd. What did she do?'

'Socked the copper round the mug with that wire basket of earth that used to have flowers in it. They were like wild animals. I don't know what would have happened if

37

the police car hadn't gone past. It took three blokes to get them through the doors.'

'What a diabolical mix-up,' I say. 'Poor old Dad. He was only trying to do his best, wasn't he? It's quite touching really.'

'Yes,' says Sid. 'Blood is thicker than water and your old man is thicker than both. Don't worry. You can make it up to him when we get the camping site organised. A nice little holiday by the sea is what they both need. It'll set them up a treat.'

It occurs to me that for once in his life Sid is right. Mum and Dad do deserve some sort of perk after their brave but misguided attempt to save me from the nick. I only hope that Little Crumbling will be up their street.

'It looks nice,' says Sid as we study my old school atlas and have a cup of Rosie prior to nipping down the station and rescuing Mum and Dad – we find a file in the shelter that gets the cuffs off. 'Little Crumbling, just next to Great Crumbling. You don't know it, Timmo, do you? You were down that way once.'

Sid is referring to my experience as a Driving Instructor at Cromingham, emergent jewel of the North Norfolk. (Shortly to become an epic movie, folks!)

'I don't remember it, Sid,' I say. 'Still, I didn't get around much.'

'Huh,' says Sid. 'You were in the back seat shafting the customers, weren't you? Well, you can forget about that here. There's going to be no handy wanky on my site.'

'I should hope not!' I say. 'Handy panky would be distasteful enough. What are you planning to do Sid?'

'We'll take the car down and spend a couple of days getting the lay of the land. Apparently a Mrs Pigerty lives on the site, but being of a nomadic disposition she could easily be prepared to part with it for a few quid.'

'She's a real gyppo, is she, Sid?'

Sid's expression registers that he has taken exception to my remark. 'A Romany, please,' he says. 'Steeped in ancient laws and crafts. They're a noble people with their own language, you know. Just because they're partial to baked hedgehog for Sunday lunch there's no need to snoot your cock at them.'

'No disrespect intended,' I say. 'I've often thought how pleasant it would be wandering over the breast of the down with the reins twitching between my fingers. Faithful Dobbin snatching at a wild rose as we wade fetlock-deep through verdant pastureland. The sun bouncing off the brightly painted shell of the caravan, the blackened cooking pot swinging lazily beside my earhole. The sweet smell of newly mown hay wafting—'

'All right! All right!' shouts Sid. 'Blimey! Are you after an Arts Council grant or something?'

'Just trying to get in the mood,' I say. 'Honeysuckle twisting round the porch and all that.'

'Don't start again,' pleads Sid. 'We'll go and collect your Mum and Dad and set off tomorrow. Should take us about three hours, I reckon.'

In fact it is not easy to get Mum and Dad away from the rossers. Not because they don't want to let them go, but because Dad barricades himself in his cell and refuses to come out. As we come through the door we hear him shouting about a 'fast to the death!'

'How long's he been on hunger strike?' I ask.

'He started just after he had his tea and biscuits,' says the bloke behind the desk. 'You his son are you? Any history of mental disease in the family?'

'We had a cousin who became a copper,' I say.

'Oh yes, highly whimsical,' says the bule, slamming his book shut. 'Listen, funny man. If you don't get your father out of here in ten minutes, I'll arrest the whole bleeding lot of you!'

'Where's my Mum?' I say.

'She's in with your Dad,' says the bule.

'That's nice,' says Sid. 'Family solidarity. Refused to be separated, did they?'

The copper looks a bit embarrassed. 'They couldn't be separated,' he says. He turns round and shouts through a door behind him. 'Millie! Have you found the keys to those blooming handcuffs, yet?'

It is pissing with rain most of the way up to the Norfolk coast but I don't allow my spirits to flag. A couple of days out of the Smoke with Sid footing the bills is not to be sniffed at and I wonder where he has it in mind for us to stay, I hope we don't have to share the same bedroom. You always get a few funny glances and one of the waiters rubbing his knee against you when he ladles out the brown windsor.

'I'm looking forward to a bit of grub,' I say, trying to raise the subject discreetly.

'There should be some chocolate in the glove compartment,' says Sid. 'That's if Jason hasn't eaten it.'

'I'm not quite certain whether he has or not,' I say, examining the stomach-turning mess sticking to the 1955 AA Book.

'Don't throw it out of the window,' says Sid. 'It's perfectly eatable once its firmed up again. You just want to make sure you don't get a bit of silver paper against your fillings.'

'I see there's a hotel at Great Crumbling,' I say. 'Got a couple of rosettes and a lift for invalid chairs.'

'Yes,' says Sid. 'We should be turning off about here. Do you notice how the air has changed?'

'I think they must be spraying that field,' I say.

'I didn't mean that!' says Sid. 'I was referring to the fact that it's fresh. No smoke, no diesel fumes. We're going to become new men out here. You know how healthy people look when they come back from their holidays? We're going to be like that all the time.'

'They're skint when they come back from their holidays, too,' I say.

Sid waves his arms into the air and nearly drives into a field of sugar beet. 'There you go again. Money! That's all you bleeding think about. Why don't you put it behind you and look at the skyline?'

'I'm sorry, Sid,' I say. 'I'll probably feel better when we've checked in at the hotel.' I wait hopefully but Sid tightens his grip on the wheel and gazes through the windscreen with a new sense of purpose.

'Did you see that signpost?' he says. 'Little Crumbling two and a half miles. It was two miles at the signpost before that. You can tell we're in the country.'

'I think I'll have a bath,' I say. 'Then a pot of tea in my room. And maybe a few rounds of hot buttered toast.'

Sid shoves on the anchors. 'That sounds handy,' he says.

'Oh good,' I say. 'Maybe I'll have a few teacakes as well.'

'I meant that,' says Sid.

I follow his nod and tilt my head to read a lop-sided sign which says 'Bitter Vetch Farm. Visitors taken in. No travellers'. Beyond the sign is a muddy track leading to a cluster of delapidated barns surrounding a building with a moulting thatched roof.

'I don't think they still do it,' I say. 'It looks deserted.'

'It can't be,' says Sid. 'There's smoke coming from the roof.'

'Maybe it's on fire?' I say hopefully.

'Looks very authentic to me,' says Sid. 'You'll get your food straight off the land there. It was just what you were talking about.'

'Should be cheap as well,' I say.

'I hadn't thought of that,' says Sid.

'No, of course not,' I say. 'I wonder you didn't bring a sleeping bag.'

Sid's eyes narrow thoughtfully and I wish I had kept my mouth shut. 'You could stretch out in the back underneath the tiger skin rug,' he says. 'Mind your feet on the upholstery and don't try and pee out of the window.'

'Sounds very tempting, Sid.' I say. 'But I'll give it a miss if you don't mind.'

The farmyard has half a dozen bedraggled chickens picking their way round it and if their condition is an example of the fare available at Bitter Vetch Farm it is difficult to see why they should want to hang around, let alone us. Sid however does not seem to notice that they look like long-necked canaries and knocks boldly on the door. There is a moment's pause and the door is opened by a comfortable Mum-type lady with flour all over her hands. These she wipes on the sheep which is lying on the kitchen table.

'Good afternoon, madam,' says Sid briskly. 'I believe you take people in?'

The woman's face hardens. 'If you'm from the Milk Marketing Board you can take your long snouts off our farm! The water in them churns came through the roof. My Dan would never knowingly cheat anyone. He ain't got the sense.'

'No madam,' says Sid. 'You misunderstand me. My assistant and I are not from the Milk Marketing Board. We would merely like to put it up here – I mean, put up here for a couple of days.'

Sid's slip of the tongue may be occasioned by the sudden appearance of a bird of about seventeen carrying a couple of pails on a yoke. This is not an easy thing to do when you are indoors and one of the pails knocks the sheep off the table. It runs out of the door bleating.

'Careful with them slops, Dimity,' says the older woman.

'Why can't you throw them out of the window like your father?'

'I've never thrown my father out of the window, mother,' says the girl. 'You be confusing me with Old Mother Gurdy. She threw Dad out of the window when he—'

'Oh lawks a mercy, do stop prattling on, gal,' says Dimity's mum. ''Twas an easy mistake to make in the dark – and no harm done with your father landing on his head. Take the gentlemen's effects up to their chamber and show them where the torch is in case they want to go to the privy.'

I am not really listening to the old bird because I am busy clocking Dimity. She wears a flared skirt falling nearly to the ground and a low cut blouse with puffed sleeves and an untied piece of ribbon dangling down beneath her creamy knockers. There is an unspoiled innocence about her that I feel like spoiling and when I stare into her soft brown eyes I feel that I may be standing on the threshold of something beautiful. She reminds me of the Ovaltine girl in wellies.

Sid makes the introductions and I learn that we are staying with Dan and Doris Dropwort who have farmed in these parts for many years. 'Dan be out with his sow now,' says Mrs Dropwort. 'You know, there be times when I think he loves that pig more than me.'

'I'm certain it's only a phase he's going through,' says Sid. 'Timmy, get the bags in, will you?'

I do wish that Sid would stop acting like Mr Big the minute we are in company but in this instance I don't say anything because Dimity puts down her yoke and comes out with me. 'You be from London, be you?' she says admiringly. 'My uncle, he been there. He went up for the Smithfield Show.'

'Oh,' I say, trying to appear interested. 'Did he win anything?'

'He got highly commended,' says the girl. 'But his pig didn't get nothing.'

'Tough,' I say. 'Do you like living out here?'

I open the car door and she immediately reaches forward for my Chelsea hold-all revealing a pleasing bulge in the bristol department. 'It's all right,' she says. 'Bit quiet. I wouldn't mind a little excitement.' She turns round and presses the bag against my chest. 'Tonight's the night I have my bath.'

'What are you doing out there, Dimity?' says an accusing voice from the doorway.

'Just getting the bags in, Ma.'

Mother and daughter are reunited on the threshold and I follow them into the house thoughtfully. Maybe Bitter Vetch Farm is not such a disaster area after all.

'What kind of time do you eat?' says Sid to Doris Dropwort when I get inside.

'Just the ordinary Wild Thyme,' says the good lady. 'Boiled up with a smidgeon of Bastard Toadflax and some Stinkweed. That do you all right, will it?'

'Without a shadow of a doubt I should think,' says Sid. 'Right Timmo, let's check out the accommodation.'

Mrs Dropwort holds up a restraining hand. 'One thing I should have asked,' she says. 'Neither of you fine gentlemen are travellers, are you? My Dimity's at a very impressionable age and we had a spot of trouble once. I don't think I could restrain my Dan if it happened again.'

'Have no fear, madam,' says Sid. 'We're buying, not selling. Mr Dropwort will have no cause for aggro – apart from agro-culture, of course. Ha, ha!'

Dimity and her mum look at each other and Sid is still fuming as we go up the creaking stairs. 'Haven't got much sense of humour, have they?' he says.

'You chose the place, Sid,' I say. 'What do you want to do now?'

'Leave our bags and take a shufti at the site,' he says. 'I can't wait to see what it's like.'

'Me neither,' says Dimity catching my eye. 'If one of you gentlemen would mind opening the door I'll bring your bags in.'

'We're sharing, are we?' I say, trying to keep the disappointment out of my voice.

'Have to, I'm afraid,' says Dimity. 'We're waiting for the builders at the moment.'

Sid opens the door and I see that a heavy brass bedstead dominates the room. There is a washstand and on it a flower patterned china basin containing a jug. Three chamberpots are littered round the floor.

'I can see what she meant about showing us to our chamber,' says Sid.

'Don't move them,' says Dimity. 'It looks like rain.'

'Not in this one it doesn't,' says Sid. 'Doesn't anyone ever empty them?'

'They're there to catch the drips,' says Dimity.

'I think the whole place is here to catch drips,' says Sid looking away from the damp patches in the ceiling. 'Come on, Timmo. Maybe you were right. Let's—'

'I'm beginning to warm to the place, Sid,' I say. 'It's oozing with character and it seems a shame to move when everybody has been so kind.' I catch Dimity's eye again and I never saw a clearer invitation to a game of stab the poker-choker. She blows through her lips when she looks at me and I only hope that Percy is not making his feelings clear to the world. You don't like to glance down unless you give the game away.

'Is the bed aired?' says Sid.

'The last couple didn't have no complaints,' says Dimity. 'I'll put Mum's warming pan in if you like. Mind you, I'll have to wait until she's finished cooking the supper in it.'

Sid lifts the cover and looks down the bed. 'Does a lot of cheese dishes, does she?' he says.

'I think it's very charming,' I say, looking round the room. 'It's a shame so many of these old places are being pulled down.'

'They're not being pulled down, they're falling down!' says Sid bitterly. 'Right, if you'll just show us where the toilet is we'll start doing our business.'

'Certainly,' says Dimity, stepping to the window. 'It's over there, just to the right of the pigsties.'

'Just to the right of the pigsties?' repeats Sid.

'That's right,' says Dimity. 'You'll have to be careful you don't step in anything.'

'Round the pigsties?' I ask.

'No, in the toilet,' says Dimity. 'Somebody took one of the bricks from under the Elsan and—'

'Don't bother,' says Sid. 'Just tell me one thing. Where did you buy your Wellington boots?'

Sid is very tight-lipped on the drive to Little Crumbling and only opens his mouth to blame me for not reminding him to pack his bicycle clips. I try and point out how nice the sugar beet looks at this time of year but he does not seem to be interested.

'Might as well give it one night,' I say artfully. 'Then if you still don't like it we can check in at that place at Great Crumbling. The Beacons, I think it was called – oh, look, there's the sea.'

'Where?' says Sid.

'Where that horizontal grey line gets darker,' I say. 'Just below that mass of low cloud. Running from East to West – or West to East. It doesn't make much difference.'

'You're trying to make it sound depressing, aren't you?' says Sid. 'Once the leaves come out and the sun starts shining it's going to look quite different.'

'Spring is a bit late up here,' I observe.

'They get theirs from Scandanavia, don't they?' says Sid. 'Stands to reason it's going to be a bit late. Ask this geezer where the Pigertys hang out.'

'The bloke with the smock and the straw hanging out of his hooter?' I say. 'He doesn't look as if he knows what month it is.'

'There's nobody else about,' says Sid. 'Except that bloke tying the bow round the pig's neck outside the pub.'

'Welcome to the carnival, gentlemen,' says the bloke in the smock. 'How can I be of service to 'ee?'

'We're looking for the Pigertys,' I say.

An expression of hatred comes over the rustic's face. 'Gyppo filth!' he spits. 'Don't let old Dan Dropwort yonder hear you mention their name. He be dang certain they put a curse on his filberts.' We look across to where our unknowing host is now entering 'The Three Jolly Rapists' with his pig. 'You be from the ministry, be you?' says the rustic. 'You be going to reallocate them? I reckons Great Crumbling be the right place. Ha! ha!' The straw falls out of his hooter and he folds it double and debates which nostril to shove it up.

'We just want to find the Pigertys at the moment,' says Sid. 'Are we headed in the right direction?'

'Just follow your noses and you can't miss them,' says the old man. 'Branch right past the alms houses and follow the Great Crumbling Road. It be just past the beet processing plant and before you get to the naturists' sanctuary.'

'Thank Gawd,' says Sid. 'I was just waiting for him to mention the sewage works.'

'That be opposite,' says the rustic.

'Nice little place,' I say as we drive out of the village. 'I've never seen a combined chip shop and crematorium before but I suppose, with the drift from the land, you have to duplicate.'

'It wouldn't be a drift if I was here,' says Sid. 'It would be a bleeding stampede! Carnival, huh! These people have got to wake up if they're going to take advantage of the new prosperity I'm bringing to the area.'

'At least it's nice about the naturist's sanctuary,' I say. 'All the wild life and birds will be an added attraction.'

'Yes,' says Sid, gazing out of the window. 'We should be nearly there. Look for the column of smoke drifting up lazily from the camp fire.'

'There's a lot of smoke over there,' I say. 'Oh no, it's coming from a chimney. That must be the beet processing plant.

'Attractive, isn't it?' says Sid. 'Functional yet not without a certain stark grandeur. The grey goes very well with the sky, too.'

'Uhm,' I say. 'I don't fancy that dump, though.' I am staring at a pile of rusting engine parts which are strewn across a sea of mud as if distributed by an explosion. The gutted chassis of two cars lie on their backs like dead cockroaches and a mean-looking alsatian rattles its chain hungrily. In the background is a caravan trailer with a line of washing leading to a stunted tree with most of the branches lopped off it.

'No,' says Sid. 'It's not very—' he breaks off and we both look at each other. 'You don't reckon—?'

'It must be, Sid,' I say. 'I can see the sign further on for the nature reserve. Let's scarper.'

'Hang on a minute,' says Sid. 'It's a nice little meadow and there's the sea behind it. The wind blows off the sea so the sewage works is no problem. There's a wood round the nature reserve. The Beet Processing Plant is quite harmless. Once we get the place cleaned up it could be quite handsome. We could even use some of those old cars for a kids' adventure playground.'

Say what you like about Sid but when he is in the mood no one can beat him for cock-eyed optimism. 'Sid—!' I say.

'Can't do any harm to have a look,' says my brother-in-law. 'I don't know how much they want for the place. It might be a snip.'

'The kind you get with a vasectomy,' I say. 'Forget it, Sid. I have a feeling about this place.'

'Noggett Superhols,' muses Sid. 'I can just see the sign. The happy holidaymakers running down to the sands hand in hand. It would be marvellous for Rosie and the kiddies. I don't know why I've never thought of it before. Just got my priorities wrong, I suppose. Still, I'm big enough to admit that.'

He is still rambling on to himself as we pick our way through the puddles and try to keep out of reach of the alsatian. From the way it looks at me I can see that it fancies me a bloody sight more than a tin of Pedigree Chum and I am not taking any chances.

'Right, here we go,' says Sid. 'Eyes down for the count up.'

He bangs smartly on the door of the caravan and the alsatian shows him its teeth all the way down to the gum. 'Who said "fangs ain't what they used to be"?' says Sid. He starts to double up and then stares at me accusingly. 'Don't you get it?' he says.

'Just because I don't laught it doesn't mean I don't get it,' I say.

'Who isn't getting it?' The voice is not Sid's but belongs to the bird who has just opened the door. By the cringe! What a banquet for the mince pie. I suck in breath so quickly that her diaphanous black nightie moves a couple of inches in my direction. The last time I saw anything like it was in one of those 'Harem-style pyjama set' ads. She has dark flashing eyes to go with her barnet, and a scarlet, glistening north and south that pouts temptingly. I don't know how long her eye-lashes are but they could break your fall from a first story window. As for her Bristol Cities, they are definitely not second division material and the rake on them makes you feel that you are being covered by a couple of revolvers.

'Yes,' says Sid, his mouth hanging open like a tear in an armpit. 'I mean, good afternoon, Miss. We've come from Madame Necroma.'

The bird turns her head over her shoulder. 'Fantasia, the gobos are here,' she calls.

'Gobos?' says Sid. 'Doesn't sound very nice.'

'Probably some kind of Romany expression,' I say, once again revealing that deep fund of general knowledge that used to make me a natural for the St Luke's Youth Club quiz team – why they didn't pick me I will never understand. They have their own language, you know.'

'Oh yes,' says Sid. 'I've heard of that. "Dogging". It means watching people having it off in cars, doesn't it? I suppose it makes a change from television – well, not so much these days.'

'What is it Esmeralda? Have the beauteous ones arrived as foretold by Aunty Rhoda.' The latest bird on the scene must be the sister of the first one and is wearing a shiny black dressing gown with signs of the zodiac all over it. She is no inferior in knockout good looks to Esmeralda and I temporarily forget Dimity and her bed warmer.

'How did they know we were coming?' whispers Sid. 'There's no telephone and a letter would take weeks to get here even if Madame Necroma could organise a whip round and buy a stamp.'

'Do not inquire too deeply into the secrets of the Romanies, oh furnace of desire,' says Fantasia. 'We have ways of transmitting things that are beyond the comprehensive of ordinary shotfots. It was foretold that you would come in the Book of Toads and here you are. Come with me to the coupling chamber.'

'Blimey!' says Sid. 'This is a bit sudden, isn't it? I mean, I know I'm irresistible but usually birds manage to hang on for a couple of minutes before the inevitable happens.'

'We Romanies are not like other polducks,' says Esmeralda, suddenly reaching out her arms to draw us into the caravan. 'We have fire in our veins not blood.'

'Must be terrible when you have heartburn,' says Sid. 'Look, I'm comforted by your very natural response to my magnetism but I really came here because Madame Necroma said that you might be interested in selling your field. Are your Mum or Dad about?'

'They're out collecting antiques,' says Esmeralda, digging her nails into my arm. 'Oh, how can you farrowblat about business when the stoats are dancing?'

'Well,' I say. 'When you put it like that it does seem a bit, sort of – er—'

'There's nobody in, then?' says Sid.

'Not yet,' says Fantasia. She opens her robe and gives Sid a flash of the full frontals. Not a stitch can be seen that does not belong to the seams of her gown.

'Yes,' says Sid. 'Well, maybe you could . . .'

His voice dies away as Fantasia rises up on tip-toe and plucks open her gown so that she can wrap it round Sid's body. 'You are my graunchy,' she says and kisses him gently on the lips.

Phew! It is a sight to warm the cock-holes of your tart and I soon realise that Esmeralda has succumbed to the magic that is building up. Her scarlet cakehole glides toward mine and her fingers play the Crumpet Voluntary on the front of my trousers. 'Did you really know we were coming?' I ask.

'I can always tell when someone is coming,' says the

bird starting to nibble my ear. 'It runs in the family.'

Like a bleeding torrent! I think to myself. Blimey, what a couple of ravers. They have gone off faster than a cargo of Vietnamese snoek. Can it really be that they reckon us rigid, or is there more to it than that? I hate to be a suspicious of a bird who is exercising her digits in such an agreeable fashion but these days you have to be careful, don't you?

I look round to see what Sid is doing and find that he is dining lightly off one of Fantasia's knockers. She has his hampton out and is juggling with his balls like she is trying to count a handful of loose change with one hand. Goodbye, Sid. I can forget about him if it is a case of restraint being shown.

'There's not much room in here is there?' I say.

'We'll have to share a bit,' says the bird. I get the idea what bit she is talking about when she rubs her fuzz up against my hampton like she is trying to put a shine on the nob at the bottom of the bannisters. 'I'll get on the stove,' she says.

Before I can ask what she is about, she has stepped out of her baggy, see-through lounging trousers and hitched her fife on to the flat surface of the electric oven. 'Come on,' she says. 'It's just the right height. I can rest the back of my legs against your chest.'

Oh dear. Life is a constant struggle, isn't it? In my heart of hearts I know that no good will come of this encounter but I am powerless to stop myself. As far as Percy is concerned, this is one bit of inflation that Dennis Healey will never conquer. I look down and the curse of the Leas is standing out proudly like the prow of a lugger – I said, lugger, lads. Let's have no slip ups at the printers, please.

'Bring him here, dear.' Esmeralda has also copped an eyeful of the plus feature and she pulls up the top half of her nightie to reveal a thicket in which it would be a pleasure to picket. 'You know where it goes, don't you?'

'Of course,' I say. 'Where you've just put it.'

Honestly! This girl must be a whiz at Racing Demon. Her fingers swoop down like hungry hawks and my dick has been dunked in the dilly pot before you can say Donald Duck. And what a delightful feature it is, too. A grip firmer than an insurance agent's hand shake and a tremble like Enoch Powell clocking the title of 'Black Beauty'. Just a few thrusts and I can see that I am going to have my work cut out to avoid breaking the British all comer's record. Always one to try and give total satisfaction, I suspend motion and send my mits down to indulge in a spot of skin diving. Round the base of my immersed mad mick I delicately dust my digits along the length of the clit slit and feel a current of warmth expand through my orchestras.

'Yes!' gasps Esmeralda. 'There! Keep doing it—'

'AAAARGH!' Regular readers might think that I am giving vent to a primitive love yodel coincidental with a vote of thanks and farewell to a few hundred thousand old friends, but this is not the case. My knob was clearly not the only one to be turned on and in my efforts to please I have just started to grill my balls on the hot plate. Esmeralda has also copped a few thousand educated volts up her backside and the two of us rise like rockets before landing in an untidy heap which includes the contents of a dish rack, a bread bin and half a dozen eggs.

'Flaming joggos!' I look up, terrified, and see an enormous bearded geezer filling the door of the caravan. He has a gold ring through one of his earholes and his swarthy face is contorted in anger. 'You swine!' he grits. 'Molesting my little girls.'

Sid falls off one of the bunks and dives through a door at the end of the caravan. An ironing board falls on his head and he reels back half-stunned.

'It's all right, Daddy,' says Fantasia. 'These gentlemen want to buy the field.'

'By the coggies!' The bearded one grinds his teeth together with a sound like half a ton of slate changing position in the hold of a tramp steamer. 'They'd better be prepared to pay a good price for it!'

CHAPTER THREE

In which Sid becomes the owner of a seaside field for which
he has great plans and in which Timmy tiptoes along a
corridor towards an appointment with ecstasy.

'Oh my Gawd,' says Sid. 'That bloke made the Mafia seem
like a building society.'

'We were taken for a ride,' I say. 'The whole thing was
a put up job.'

'It may have been in your case,' says Sid. 'Nobody had
to put mine up. Oh dear, what an experience. These
gyppos certainly have something. Did you notice that when
her snalgo closed round your dinker—'

'My bladgers went all flumspurgle? Yes, I did notice
that, Sid. But it doesn't alter the fact that we got done.
How much did you have to pay in the end?'

'I don't know,' says Sid. 'I haven't worked it out yet.
Not with the free grazing rights and the wart charming. I
told him he'd have to wait for most of the money.'

'Like the rest of us,' I say. 'Oh Sid, when will you ever
learn? Those birds were clearly up to no good – up to page
one hundred and fifty in the "Kama Sutra", definitely.
But good? Never!'

'All right, all right!' says Sid. 'The important thing is
that we've got the place – more or less, anyway. Once a
few legal details have been ironed out.'

'What he said was that unless he gets the money he's
going to stamp on your didiwodgers,' I say. 'And I don't
think he meant your National Savings Book.'

'Don't keep on,' says Sid. 'We'll start worrying about
that in the morning. Let's take a look round the property
now.'

Our conversation is taking place at a spot half way between the pile of scrap metal – some of which is now being loaded on to a clapped out lorry and the cliff edge. Dusk is falling slightly faster than my spirits and my balls are still stinging. Not from the hot plate but from the ferrule of Mrs Pigerty's umbrella. She was a very short tempered lady and took after her old man – with an axe, on several occasions, I later heard from the caretaker at the beet processing plant.

'Blimey, I hope the beach is good ,' I say. 'Remember how you were going to have a thorough recce before you let yourself in for anything?'

Sid looks as if he is just about to say something when there is a loud 'crump!' noise and the sign on the edge of the cliff disappears. 'Crikey!' breathes Sid. 'A cliff fall. That's not very nice.'

Behind us there is the sound of gears grinding and I see Fantasia waving two fingers from the window as the caravan lurches forward out of the mud.

'They're not wasting any time, are they?' says Sid.

'No,' I say. Feelings of unease are not strangers to my body at this time and I stride purposefully towards the cliff edge. Could it be that there is something less than a thousand per cent satisfactory about the proposed site for 'Superhols'? Feeling the ground in front of me carefully I edge forward, expecting at any moment to be soaked to the skin by the spume from giant waves pounding against the foot of the cliffs. To my surprise, when I look down, there is actually a beach. What is more it has sand on it. Not a lot, but enough to break up the monotony of the shingle and the fallen earth from the cliff face. Sid appears beside me and picks up a stone which he holds over the edge of the cliff. He extends his free arm so that he can examine his watch and pauses before dropping the stone. 'Right,' he says, waiting until the stone has struck the beach. 'Three seconds from the sea.'

'You're going to print that in the advertisements, I suppose?' I say. 'Honestly, Sid. Have you no spark of human decency?'

'Better check it, I suppose,' says Sid. He picks up another stone and drops it over the cliff. There is a blinding flash, a deafening roar, and a column of earth and stones begins to patter down around our nuts.

'Be another of them mines,' says a familiar voice. 'Best thing for cleaning your ears, a fresh turnip.'

We turn and see our friend from the village green clutching one of the aforementioned vegetables. From the look of his smock it appears that he has fallen over several times on the way to the field.

'Mines?' says Sid.

'A plague of them along the coast around here,' says the yokel. 'Left over from the war. The beach between the Crumblings be littered with them.'

'Where *is* Great Crumbling?' I ask.

The rustic points towards the western horizon. 'Out there,' he says. 'Where Little Crumbling'll be in a few years.'

'Underneath the sea!' says Sid.

'Ar,' replies the rustic. 'They do say that when the sea be calm you can hear the church bell ringing. But I say they be crazy who say that.' He gives a loud maniacal laugh and the turnip falls out of his ear.

Sid makes as if he is going to hurl another stone at the beach and then thinks better of it. 'That's marvellous, isn't it?' he says. 'A minefield and the bleeding land disappearing under your feet. He never said anything about that!' He turns angrily towards the entrance to the field through which the pick-up truck is now leaving in pursuit of the caravan.

'He wouldn't, would he?' I say. 'That's why his caravan is pulled by a bleeding Cadillac.'

'You sent 'em packing, I see,' says the yokel gleefully. 'I knew you be ministry men the moment I clapped eyes on 'ee.'

'Piss off!' says Sid. 'Otherwise I'll lose your turnip for you.'

'Must be erosion,' I say, looking down the front of the cliff. 'They have a lot of it round here.'

'It's ridiculous,' says Sid. 'The bleeding country is small enough as it is.'

'I don't think it works like that,' I say. 'What the sea takes away from one side of the country, it puts back on the other.'

'Blimey,' says Sid. 'We should have bought something in Wales. In a few hundred years it would be big enough to graze cattle on. I don't know why everybody isn't doing it.'

'They don't have your foresight,' I say. 'Shall we get back to the farm now? I'm feeling a bit peckish.'

'Good idea,' says Sid. 'You need an early night with all those mines to shift in the morning.'

I pretend I haven't heard what he said and we go back to the farm with a fine drizzle falling – when I think about it it is the finest thing I have seen since arriving at Little Crumbling.

'I must ask you to avert your eyes as you go through the scullery,' says Doris Dropwort. 'Dimity be having her bath.'

I immediately glance through the open door and clock the fetching form of Mrs Dropwort's firstborn waving to me from a large tin tub in front of the fire. 'Ma,' she calls, making only a token attempt at shielding her milk-white mammaries from my piercing orbs. 'I don't think much to these bath crystals. They don't grant no favours to the snout.'

'Oh, dang my withers, gal,' says Doris. 'You be a stupid ha'pworth and no mistake. These be your father's sheep dip powders. You bain't got the liver fluke.'

'I wondered what these bloody sheep were doing everywhere,' says Sid. 'Get out of it!'

'Keep the doors shut,' says Doris. 'We don't want them upstairs again.'

'That explains the marks on the counterpane,' says Sid. 'Oh my Gawd. This is incredible. You mean to tell me that you dip the sheep in the family bath water?'

'They don't come to no harm,' says Mrs Dropwort. 'Anyroad, a little lamb makes a lovely loofah.' Further discussion on the subject is interrupted by high pitched honking and squealing noises from the yard. 'Ah, there be Dan,' says Mrs Dropwort. 'Let's see if he's run over something for supper.'

She goes to the door and I exchange another glance with Dimity. After my spot of caught-us interrupted I am eager to put the record straight and the expression on the bird's face definitely does not say 'reject'. I must get rid of Sid and find out where her bedroom is. He is already starting to yawn and I reckon the country air is going to see him off in no time.

'Oh dear, I be a daft mullock. I dropped the soap.' The little temptress is casting her Manchesters over the side of the tub like they are fenders and I step forward to do my duty as an English gentleman. Eager not to offend the senior Dropworts, I collect the soap and step forward with my hand over my eyes. 'Yaaaah!' Splash! A bloody sheep has to get in the way, doesn't it? I take a header into the tub and when I get my waterlogged nut out from between Dimity's legs it is to see Dan Dropwort and his pig glaring down at me with thunder in their eyes.

'Who said you could wash your hair in my daughter's bath water?' storms the human half of the duo. 'There's

Mabel got to go into that.' Before he can say another word, the pig snorts and scrambles into the bath sending a tidal wave of water across the kitchen. 'They make a pretty picture, don't they?' says Farmer Dropwort grudgingly. 'My two girls at their toilet.'

'He's a funny bloke, that,' says Sid when we get upstairs. 'Fancy letting the pig sit in the armchair.'

'It did get his slippers,' I say.

'Yeah, but then it ate them,' says Sid. 'It seems a bit strange to me.'

'It was angry because he wouldn't give it another mug of elderberry wine,' I say.

'God knows why,' says Sid. 'Did you taste that stuff? I suddenly found he'd given me a second helping'

'That wasn't him, that was me.' I say. 'I slipped mine into your glass when you were helping pull his gumboots off.'

'Thanks a bundle,' says Sid. 'I'll do you a good turn one day. What side of the bed do you want?'

'Oh, I'm easy,' I say casually. 'Nearest the door – I mean, the wall.'

'Handy if you're taken short, I suppose,' says Sid. 'I hope you brought a pair of stilts to walk across the yard.' He rubs his hands together and shivers. 'Blooming draughty in here, isn't it? Have you noticed how the drips are being blown away from the poes?'

'I haven't been yet,' I say.

'I mean the drips from the ceiling,' says Sid. 'Gordon Bennett, you are thick sometimes. Move your khyber off that bed and let's get downstairs. Perhaps some of that stew will warm me up.'

But when we get round the kitchen table we find that the stew is for Mabel. She scrambles on to a chair beside Sid and I have never seen such disgusting manners in my

60

life. Snout down, food flying everywhere; loud, smelly belches— the pig isn't much better.

'I hope you like fish fingers,' says Doris Dropwort. 'I only opened the packet last Friday.' She brushes something off the plate in front of her. 'That reminds me. You must renew the wire mesh in the food cupboard, Dan.'

'You don't have a fridge?' I ask, wondering whether it was my imagination when I thought I saw something dart under the leaf of my aptly named Stinkweed.

'Freezes out the natural goodness,' says Farmer Dropwort shortly. 'When you have one of nature's treasures like a fish finger you don't want to spoil it, do 'ee? Bain't that so m'dear?' One might think that he would be addressing his wife with this remark but it is the pig that receives a chuck under the chin.

I shoot a sidelong glance at Dimity but she is busy cleaning up her plate with a piece of bread. Dad usually does this after he has got some nosh on it but I expect that Dimity knows best. I have a quick poke at the fish finger and then start forming it together in a tight ball with the greens so that it looks as small as possible when I push it to the side of the plate and try and hide it under the knife and fork. I don't want to hurt Mrs Dropwort's feelings but even Mum's fish fingers had white bits in the middle.

'You ate that quick, lad,' says Dan. 'Good country fare obviously appeals to the lad, Doris. Fill his plate for 'e.'

'No,' I say. 'It's—' But too late. My plate is buried in Bastard Toadflax and fish finger nails.

'You want to watch that washing of the hair,' warns Dan. 'Too much of it weakens the noddle. Look at old Walter Looney you was talking to on the village green today. He was never the same once he started washing.'

'I didn't notice he washed,' says Sid.

'Ah,' says Dan. 'He stopped, but by then it was too late.'

'A lot of young people today wash,' says Dimity. 'There bain't be no harm in it.'

'Shut your gabbler when your father's holding forth to the gen'lemen!' says Doris angrily. 'He knows what's best for us and the pig.'

'Meddlessome old fool,' says Dan, ignoring the interruptions and thoughtfully stroking Mabel who is now resting her head on his plate.' I 'spect he wanted to know all your business?'

'Who? Walter Looney?' says Sid. 'Oh yes. He thought we were from the ministry.'

'No respect for people's privacy,' says Dan. 'Thought you were from the ministry. Typical.' He waits expectantly and looks at Sid.

'But we're not,' says Sid.

'Ah!' says Dan. 'So you must be something else?'

'That's right,' says Sid.

'Something not connected with the ministry?'

'Very definitely,' says Sid.

Dan continues to gaze searchingly at Sid and then, receiving no further answer, turns to his wife. 'Have our visitors filled in the forms, yet?' he says.

'What forms?' says Sid.

'Just routine,' says Dan. 'Name, address, occupation. Be you from the other side of Norwich?'

'Of course!' says Sid.

'Right. Then nationality as well,' says Dan.

During this interchange, I have taken the opportunity to slide my knee sideways and give Dimity's leg a sensual nudge. 'Be off with you, you woolly varmint!' she cries.

'Ssh! It's me.' I whisper.

'I thought it was one of the sheep,' she says. 'What be you up to? Be you fruity of I?' The idea is clearly not unappealing to her because she slides her foot towards mine and begins to rub it against the table leg so hard that Sid's plate starts to tremble.

'I be,' I murmur. 'My leg's over here.'

She shoots a quick glance at her dad and slides her hand under the table. Percy trembles expectantly and – 'ouch!' I wish she had put her fork down first. My knees hit the underside of the table and all the Stinkweed pods roll off Dad Dropwort's knife.

'Give's you energy, don't it, son?' he says. 'Give him some more, Doris. The lad looks as if he needs building up.'

But fortunately, Mabel having finished up all her stew has turned her attention to the fish fingers and is licking up the remains of the tureen. Seconds later, she is violently sick in one of Dan's Wellington boots. Sid shudders and starts to fill in the form that Ma Dropwort has shoved in front of him. Dan is a real nosy old git because he cranes over and peers eagerly at what Sid is writing.

'Entrepreneur?' he says. 'What be that? I ain't never heard o' that afore.'

'It means a bloke who undertakes things,' says Sid. 'I've dabbled in many fields in my time.'

'Why don't you write that down then?' says Dan. 'Undertaker – and you won't be able to use the fields round here. Vicar say it be the graveyard or nothing.'

'Oh Gawd,' says Sid.

'You won't get rich round here, boy,' says Dan. 'There bain't many that kicks the bucket in these parts.'

'You amaze me,' says Sid, pushing away his plate. 'Thank you Mrs Dropwort. That was-er-very-um—'

He looks at me for help and I quickly stack his plate on top of mine. 'Just like my Mum's cooking,' I say.

Sid looks relieved. 'Exactly,' he says. 'I couldn't have put it better myself. Ah well, time to turn in, I think. This country air certainly gets through to you, doesn't it?'

'You don't want to listen to the radio?' says Mrs Dropwort. 'We always have the nine o'clock news before we turn in.'

'Not tonight, thank you,' says Sid. 'I think I'll give myself a treat and just imagine a couple of natural disasters and a large investment trust collapsing.'

He rises to his feet, yawning, and I quickly turn my head and whisper in the lovely Dimity's earhole, 'Where be your – where's your bedroom?'

'Down the end of the corridor,' she murmurs. 'Next to the ferrets.'

'I'll see you later,' I hiss. I give her a quick wink and she flutters her lips at me in a way that puts a crinkle in my winkle. What a little darling. If she does not come across with the good things of life I will never trust my eye for a quick Friar Tuck again. She is all pink and scrubbed and her lips are glistening in the soft light thrown by the oil lamp. Soon I will be harvesting the rich fruit of her knockers and ploughing the furry furrow with my mingle wurzel. Gor! I can hardly keep from rubbing my hands together as I follow Sid up the creaking stairs.

'It's funny,' he says. 'We haven't done much today but I'm dead knackered.'

'You'll feel better after a good night's sleep,' I say soothingly.

'I need something good after that meal,' says Sid. 'I thought your mum was a diabolical cook till I tasted those fish fingers.' He starts peeling off his clobber and I feel the water in the jug on the washstand. Blimey! If it was any colder it would have ice on it. I don't fancy dunking my dick in that. I had better wait till Sid is in bed anyway, otherwise he will smell a rat.

'Blast!' he says. 'I fancy a piss but I'm buggered if I'm walking across that yard.'

'Use one of the pots,' I say. 'That's what they were made for.'

'Must have been terrible when they invented karsis,' muses Sid. 'Imagine it. You're sitting on top of the chamber pot business and suddenly – bang, smash, wallop! Nobody wants them any more. What do you tell your wife?'

'You say the bottom has dropped out of the market,' I say.

'It's impossible to have a serious conversation with you, isn't it?' says Sid shaking his head sadly. 'I try and touch upon an issue if vital human interest and you immediately become frivolous.' He finishes having his pee and carries the jerry over to the window. 'You want to think about other people's predicaments a bit more.' He forces up the window and empties the potty into the night. There is an angry shout and a volley of rustic oaths. 'Sorry, Mr Dropwort,' shouts Sid. 'Just drips from the ceiling.'

He hurries into bed and I am alarmed to see that the whole contraption sinks so that his bum is barely off the floor. It is more like a hammock than a bed. I don't fancy spending a night with him in that. Still, with a bit of luck, I won't have to. I wait till he has stopped threshing about and quickly slip out of my jeans and underpants. Now for the moment of truth. Dimity has had her bath so I can hardly falter in my personal freshness programme. I work up a brave lather in the freezing water and take a deep breath. Ouch! Before my very eyes, percy shrinks to half his normal size as he cops the suds. What I berk I am. I should just have slapped on some of Sid's after shave lotion. I don't fancy it on my face but it is OK for annointing the nether regions. Still, now I am under way I might as well do a job that would win the approval of the British Medical Association – should there be any of its members still left in the country.

'Are you coming to bed?' says Sid's muffled voice.

'Won't be a sec,' I say. 'Just cleaning my Ted's.' I pick up Sid's after shave and then think better of it. It could be nasty if he caught a whiff of the niff and thought it was for his benefit. I shiver at the thought and put on the clean pair of Y-fronts I was keeping for the journey home. I hope Dimity is going to be grateful. This kind of preparation could earn me a date with Princess Grace of Monaco.

'Hurry up!' grumbles Sid. 'I can't get to sleep with the light on.'

'Do you want the window left open?' I ask.

'No,' says Sid. 'But we haven't got much alternative. The top half fell out when I emptied the jerry.'

I put Sid's after shave near the door and extinguish the lamp. I don't fancy getting into bed with Sid but maybe the very fact that I don't coco the idea reveals something disturbing about my hormone balance. I mean, do I dislike the idea because deep down inside I am drawn towards it? Do I secretly fancy Sid? When I think about it, I don't have any close mates and it can't be the money that keeps me tagging along with his ridiculous schemes. It is all a bit disturbing. Perhaps all these birds are just a pretence to stop me facing up to the truth?

'What's the matter with you now?' says Sid's irritable voice.

'I'm just coming,' I say.

'That's what I thought,' says Sid. 'Having a crafty Joddrell. Didn't your dad ever have a talk with you about stunting your growth?'

I don't answer him but pull back the threadbare blankets and slide into the bed. Blimey! It goes down faster than Britain's standard of living. I have no chance of avoiding contact with Sid's body.

'Gawd! You're cold,' complains Sid. 'Boney, too.'

'At least there's a bottle,' I say. I fish it out and can just read 'Bullards Brown Ale' on the label.

'God knows who left that,' says Sid. 'I found a jar of fishpaste as well. Try and keep off me, will you?'

'I'm sorry,' I say. 'It's blooming impossible in this bed. Perhaps there's something we can put between us?'

'Or you could sleep on the floor,' says Sid.

I am about to say 'I should coco' or words to that effect when it occurs to me that the further I am away from Sid the easier it will be for me to slip out of the room undetected. I put up a lot of token rabbit and then grudgingly stretch out on the floor, piling as much clobber as I can on top of me. Sid, selfish sod that he is, is snoring before my head has collided with the pillow that I have wrested from beneath his nut. I wait until his broken breathing takes on some kind of pattern and then stretch out my arm for the after shave lotion. 'Baneful Grass' it is called. I swill some over the region of my Marquis of Lorne and – ouch! Not only baneful but painful. Still, you have to suffer for art. What is a little pain now compared with the ecstasy to come? I wish Percy felt in better nick. I don't think he has recovered from the freezing water. I must try not to think about it. In the past I have proved to myself that it is possible to shrink one's dick before going over the top. A few casual glances and a sly tug and the beloved organ gets all introverted and falls back on itself like a tug of war team when the rope breaks. A glance through Cosmopolitan can result in total paralysis. As for the centre of 'Playgirl' – forget it, I'll take up knitting. Why don't the authorities suppress that kind of thing? It's bad enough suspecting that every other geezer has a bigger one than you without being proved correct. Pull yourself together, Lea. Think positive. Dimity is clearly vastly enamelled of you and there will be no problems.

I stop trying to nudge Percy into life and transfer my

attention to the sound of Sid's breathing. He is definitely out like a British heavyweight prospect when his second flicks the towel in his face too hard. I smack a spot of the aftershave under my armpits and clamber noiselessly to my feet. There is still no sound from Sid so I start to tiptoe towards the door. This is more difficult because the boards creak something terrible. I pick my feet up high and – ugh! Put one of them down in a jerry. Knickers! I hope it is rain water. At least it feels cold enough. I set my hand on the latch and lift and pull. The door creaks open and I see that there is no light in the corridor – or perhaps I don't see that there is no light in the corridor. It is difficult to know how to put it, isn't it? I take a last butchers at the kipping Sid and draw the door to behind me. Just a few creaking paces away lies the delicious Dimity no doubt straining her lugholes into the night for sound of my coming. If this isn't the stuff of high romance I don't know what is. My jam tart is going pitter-pat, pitter-pat – and sometimes even patter-pit it is so excited – and I am trembling as I feel my way along the wall towards the end of the corridor. My fingers brush against something and – 'OW!!' What a blooming dangerous place to hang a gin trap. Thank God it is as clapped out as everything else in the Dropwort household or it would have had my fingers off. My scream echoes through the house and I freeze as I hear the creak of bedsprings.

'What be that?' says Dan Dropwort's worried voice. 'You put all the sheep in the front room didn't 'ee, Doris?'

'Course I did,' says Doris's drowsy voice. 'I reckon it only be one of the strangers nipped his nagglers in the bed springs. Go back to sleep, Dan.'

To my relief there is the sound of heavy bodies re-arranging themselves and then silence. With great difficulty, I prise open the gin trap and place it carefully on the floor. Dimity must have heard the noise and is no

68

doubt quivering with excitement. It is a pity her bedroom is next to the ferrets. It sort of takes the edge off the romance a bit. I don't know if you have ever niffed ferrets but you would not want to bottle up the pong and give it to your Aunty Madge for Christmas. The smelly little bleeders are scampering round their cage and I take great care that I don't shove any of my digits through the mesh and give them a light snack. They have wicked teeth, ferrets.

At last, the shadowy outline of the portal is revealed before me. The great moment has arrived. I wonder if her bed dips down like ours? Still, it won't be so bad rolling down on top of her. There is no light under the door and I put my hand on the knob and start to strain. It is not the only knob that is straining either. Percy is the first part of me past the door by a good few inches and the front of my Y-fronts must look as if I am smuggling flat irons. I try and get my mince pies working but it is all I can do to make out the bed.

'Dimity?' There is a rustle of anticipation and the adrenalin pumps through my body. She must have been on the point of dropping off. They seem to get their heads down pretty early in the country. I glide towards the bed and drop to my knees. How strange. I seem to be kneeling in something wet and mushy. Before I have the chance to think of an explanation, a huge object looms up before me and blots out the dim light from the window. Can this be my beloved? 'Honk! Honk!' A large, wet tongue rasps across my face and an even stronger niff cuts across the Eau de Ferret that still hangs in the air. It is Farmer Dropwort's bleeding pig! I don't know whether it reckons I am after its swill – any other explanation is too horrible to think about – but it makes a vicious lunge at me and I surrender to panic. Forgetting about the need to keep quiet, I scramble to my feet and leg it for the door. Bloody Mabel is after me and she nudges me between the scotch eggs just as I am going past the ferrets. A very disturbing experience it is, too – as the ferrets would be first to admit when their cage crashes to the floor. I am hurtling down the corridor when a door bursts open and Dropwort appears wearing a night cap and carrying a shotgun. I think it is only when a ferret runs up his leg that he decides to empty his weapon into the ceiling and a shower of plaster rains down. Dropwort leaps into the air and lands with a wild scream – he has stepped on the gin trap. Mabel butts me up the backside again and together we rocket down the rickety stairs and start racing each other round the kitchen.

It is a bit early to be certain but I reckon that the odds on me making it with Dimity tonight are lengthening to considerably worse than evens.

CHAPTER FOUR

In which Timmy gets the lay of the land and brings succour to a young mother who is frightened of being alone.

'Phew!' says Sid. 'She was a passionate little number and no mistake. Mind you, it didn't come as a complete surprise. I'd noticed the way she was looking at me. Sizing me up, so to speak. During supper especially. I could see what she had in mind.'

'Oh yes?' I say.

'Yes,' says Sid. 'It was shortly after you'd locked yourself in the cowshed – in fact, for a moment I thought it *was* you. I was just going to clock you one round the cakehole when I realised who it was. "'Ere I be," she murmurs. "Come to blunt your turnip for 'e."'

'How delightful,' I say through gritted teeth.

'It was,' says Sid. 'Now I realise why the bed was shaped like that. What a sack artist! I reckon the birds and the bees must have been told about her. It's a pity you decided to take the pig for a walk. There was plenty for everyone.'

'I didn't really fancy her,' I say. 'That whole place put the mockers on me.'

'I know what you mean,' says Sid. 'But she was stand out, she really was. When she peeled back my—'

'You don't have to go on about it!' I tell him. 'I don't unload all the dirty details on you, do I? I have a little decency and decorum. You want to try emulating me.'

'You can go to prison for that, can't you?' says Sid. 'Anyway, I'm not certain how you do it.'

'Oh belt up!' I say. 'The main thing is that it's all behind us now. Farmer Dropwort made it clear that he thought we were a bad influence on Mabel and that he never wanted us to darken his tea towels again.

'He thought *you* were a bad influence,' says Sid. 'It's funny but he was very possessive about that pig, wasn't he?'

'I don't care to think about it,' I say. I am not kidding either. I have not told Sid how I ended up squatting on a beam in the barn with a couple of Rhode Island Reds beside me. Mabel lay on her back beneath me and gazed up, ruminatively stroking her nipples with one of her trotters. It was a very strange experience.

'Right,' says Sid, shoving a couple of ear plugs into the sides of his nut. 'Now to clear those mines. I remember seeing them use a contraption like this in one of those old war films on the telly.'

'Did it work?' I ask.

'I dunno,' says Sid. 'The bloke was blown up soon after he started using it.'

'How whimsical,' I say. 'If you think I'm going to wander over that beach with a duff vacuum cleaner you've got another think coming.'

'Don't let the film influence you,' says Sid. 'He was having it off with Victor Mature's bird so it was obvious he wasn't going to last long.'

'I'm sorry, Sid,' I say. 'I'm going to have to put my foot down while I've still got one.'

'All right, all right,' says Sid. 'These ear plugs don't work, and the flex isn't long enough. We'll have to think of something else.'

He looks down at the beach and rubs his hands together thoughtfully. I must say, it is bloody parky. If the weather goes on like this I can't see anyone being daft enough to leave their telly and camp for two weeks in this sodden field. You could go mad trying to think of something to do.

Running a book on the time the next land mine went off would seem to be the best bet at the moment.

'Seems to me like a professional job, Sid,' I say. 'We ought to call up the Royal Engineers.'

'They've had thirty years to do it,' says Sid. 'Anyway, they'd probably charge for it. It's funny when you come to think of it. I never believed this country was capable of producing anything that would last thirty years. When they do, it's a bleeding land mine. What are you looking at?'

'Over there behind that dune,' I say. 'I think I saw a bird without any clothes on.'

'Where?' says Sid.

'She's gone now. She was pushing her way through the reeds.'

'She probably escaped from one of those cigar ads on the telly,' says Sid. 'Stop fooling about and help me think of a way to clear that beach of mines. It's not going to be the same for the kiddies unless we can do something.'

I don't say anything because I am still staring at the place where the naked crumpet took the strain off my eyeballs. Don't say I'm getting woman on the brain as well as everywhere else. I could have sworn I saw her. Deep-breasted, hair tumbling about her shoulders. A graceful, loping stride as if she was used to prancing about in the buff. I lean forward but all I can see is the reeds touching their toes as a force nine gale whips off the sea.

'I've got it!' says Sid. 'We'll use that old wheelbarrow.'

What he really means is: '*You* will use that old wheelbarrow.' Blooming hairy it is, too. We lash a piece of wood across the front at right angles to the wheel and from it Sid hangs lots of bits of barbed wire with scraps of metal tied to them – there is a considerable amount of barbed wire on the beach. Then we secure two long poles to the handles.

'Right!' says Sid, briskly. 'Off you go. Just push it back-

73

wards and forwards across the beach until the tide's out as far as it will go – maybe a bit further to be on the safe side. Don't worry, you won't come to any harm.'

'Where are you going?' I ask.

Sid does not answer and I have to make signs before he removes the earplugs he has just bunged into his nut. 'Sorry,' he says. 'I had them in the wrong ears last time. What were you saying?'

I repeat my question and am informed that Sid intends to start siting the ablutions. 'That's where they have a Tom Tit and wash their Germans,' he says. 'Good luck, and remember – you push the wheelbarrow. Don't drag it after you.'

Dear oh dear. What a bleeding agony it all is. Sid's idea is that the pieces of metal will spark off the mines and that the lengthened shafts on the wheelbarrow will prevent me copping the consequence. In fact I nearly die of exhaustion. The sand is wet and soft and I can hardly shove the wheelbarrow through it. By the time I have got down to the sea I am on my knees. No land mines have been revealed but I have turned up three pairs of false gnashers and a rusty thermos flask.

As if to salute my achievement, a few rays of watery sun probe the gloom and I turn my eyes towards the cliff top. Where is Sid? He has been conspicuous by his absence during my ordeal. Blimey? A naked bloke and bird are holding hands and staring down at me. They gaze at me steadily without flinching and then turn away to disappear behind the line of the cliff top. The minute they have gone I wonder if I really saw then. Perhaps I have been taking too much out of myself lately and am going round the twist.

I struggle back to the foot of the cliff and am just about to abandon the wheelbarrow when Walter Looney bobs up from nowhere. 'You'll never fly in that thing,' he says.

'Shove off, you stupid old twit!' I tell him.

'I 'eard yo' set yor cap at old Dan Dropwort's pig,' gabbles the rustic. 'News travels fast in these 'ere parts.'

'I suggest you try and imitate it,' I say. 'Why don't you piss off and darn that big hole in the front of your smock?'

'Because I don't want to have to pull it up when I go to the lah-ta,' says the old fool. 'Where be the pilot supposed to sit in this thing?'

I leave him squatting in the wheelbarrow and croaking 'vroom! vroom!' and return to where Sid is sorting out a pile of corrugated iron that was left when the Furmitys pulled out.

'All clear?' he asks, removing his earplugs. 'Well done, Timmo. Now you can give me a hand with this lot. It's quite useful what they've left. With that pig pen over there we should be able to knock up a very nice little washhouse. There's even a tap.'

'Don't we have to get permission to do all this?' I ask. 'What about the health authorities?'

'If we waited for them we'd never start,' says Sid. 'Anyway, they're certain to make some footling objection. That's the only way they can justify their existence. The important thing is to get some paying customers through the door. We can sort out any problems later.'

'Er – yes, Sid,' I say. 'You didn't notice anything strange while I was clearing the beach, did you?'

'Not really,' says Sid. 'Dropwort's pig was hanging around as if it was looking for something but I soon sent it packing. That horrible whining noise goes right through your nut. I never knew pigs could make a noise like that.'

'Didn't see anyone wandering along the clifftop?' I prompt.

'I wasn't really looking,' says Sid. 'Come on, let's get this karsi up. We need somewhere to sleep tonight.'

Honestly, I have to admit that Sid does throw himself

into his new venture. I have never known him work so hard. By nightfall we have built a framework to extend the piggery and mounted a couple of troughs to serve as communal wash basins. 'Very important, the old ablutions,' says Sid. 'This is where they all start picking each other up. A few shy glances over the dolly bags and the belly held in for the out of door shaving. Very Clint Eastwood. Hand back a bird's soap a couple of times and you're off on the slippery path to dalliance.'

'What about the other thing?' I ask.

'We'll wait till the sties have dried out and bung in a few Elsans – come to think of it, we don't need to bother with Elsans. Those oil drums will do the job.'

'They're a bit high, Sid. I wouldn't fancy perching on the edge of one of those after I'd had a few.'

'We'll have to sink them into the ground – or, better still, saw the top half off. The jagged edge will stop people kipping in there all day. You know what your Dad's like at home. Whining because someone's used the bit of the article he wanted to read.'

Sid is so full of energy that he even has time to make a sign saying 'Noggett Super Hols' which he places near the sea of mud at the gate. I reckon he is pushing it a bit but to my amazement, a car and caravan roll to a halt at the entrance just as it is getting really dark.

'What did I tell you?' says Sid. 'This place is a blooming goldmine. We haven't even advertised yet.'

'They must want to ask the way,' I say.

'Nonsense,' says Sid. 'Get over there and conduct them to berth OneA.'

I give him my pitying look but it is so dark that he cannot see it. Berth OneA! A blooming great empty field and Sid has to start dividing it into plots. I put down my stick with the burnt sausage on the end of it and squelch towards the gate. It is pretty parky now and I can't help my mind drifting back to Dimity and thoughts of her snowy white dumplings. I wish that she had made it clear that her bedroom was opposite the ferrets.

'Excuse me. Are you open?' I bend down and see that the bird leaning anxiously out of the window is definitely on bonus time in the looks department. I gaze past her for sight of hubby but there is only a baby in a carrycot on the back seat. 'I know it's a bit early in the season,' she says. 'But we thought we'd try and snatch a few days before the crowds build up.'

'Very wise,' I say. 'Er – yes. We're open. You've caught us a bit on the hop but that's all right. Just the two of you, is it?' I nod my head towards the baby.

'My husband's joining us tomorrow,' says the bird. 'He couldn't get away from the office and he sent me on ahead to avoid the traffic. I'll never do it again. Driving with this caravan is murder. I've nearly had it off three times on the way up here.'

Uuhm, I think to myself. You could have it off with me any day of the week, darling. I extend my sympathy and a couple of inches of submerged percy and start leading the bird towards the edge of the wood. The most favoured position on the site is near the cliff and next to the wood and the worst on the road next to the beet processing plant where you stand to cop first whiff of the sewage works should the wind change direction. Frankly, I don't think anyone is ever going to have to worry about that problem because I cannot see Sid getting past D4 in his berth system.

'Are we the only people here?' says the bird when I go round to see if there is anything she wants.

'There's my brother-in-law and me,' I say. 'We sleep on the site.'

'Good,' she says. 'It's a bit lonely at the moment, isn't

77

it? I'm not used to this kind of thing. My husband is the caravan fan. Oh, I do hope he wins tonight.'

I sense that the bird is eager to make conversation because she is scared of being on her own and I am only too happy to oblige with a few friendly noises. 'What's he doing?' I ask.

'North London Karate Championships,' she says. 'He's a real fanatic. Our living room at home is inches deep in brick dust. We used to have a lovely mantelpiece before he started practising his chops on it.'

'You must wish you were there,' I say.

'Not really,' says the bird. 'He's a terrible loser. If things go wrong he becomes violent – well, even more violent. He kicked the wheel off a police car once – while it was still going.'

I can't help being disappointed by the bird's description of her old man. He is definitely my least favourite type of husband. I like the meek forgiving type, preferably engaged in a potholing expedition in Western Australia. 'Still, he must be handy to have around when things get nasty,' I say.

'They usually only get nasty when he *is* around,' says the bird. 'I do hope this holiday soothes him down a bit. There, there, darling. Mummy's coming.' This last remark is addressed to the baby and I skate off to fetch a bucket of water so that Mum can heat up its bottle. I don't reckon she would fancy the plumbing arrangements as they almost stand at the moment.

'Ta,' she says. 'That's sweet of you. Put it on the side there, will you?'

'Nice little place you've got there – I mean, here,' I say clocking the curve of her fife as she bends over to rummage in the baby's hold-all. 'Very compact.'

'I suppose it's all right,' says the bird. 'It's the first time I've ever been in it apart from when Malcolm bought it.'

She looks out of the window into the darkness and gives a little shiver. 'You be round later, will you?' she says. 'I mean, to check that everything is all right?'

'Sure,' I say. 'If you hear anyone poking about, it will be me.'

'That's reassuring,' she says. 'You might pop in and have a cup of tea if I'm still up. I expect I'll read for a bit.'

'Fine,' I say. 'I'll see you later, then.' I give her my 'you can depend on me ma'am' look borrowed from the young cavalry 'lootenant' who always leads the wagon train through hostile 'Injun' territory and pat the baby on the head. It starts screaming immediately.

'He's hungry,' says the bird. 'Don't worry, Elgin. Your din dins is coming right up. Nice Mr—?'

'Lea, Timothy Lea,' I say.

'Nice Timothy Lea has got the water for you. I'm Patty Lucas by the way.'

'Pleased to meet you, Patty,' I say. I give her a second exposure to the dazzling Teds and sense that a moment of magic has occurred as she fiddles with the lid of her strained beef and vegetable broth.

'I wonder if you could do something for me,' she breathes, 'I was supposed to ring Malcolm and tell him where I was but I don't want to leave Elgin.'

'Have no fear,' I say. 'What's the number?'

'It's Finchley Town Hall,' she says. 'Give him my love if you speak to him.'

Sid is scratching at the bottom of a tin of fruit salad when I get back to the fire. 'I've left you the pineapple segments,' he says, tilting back the tin and guzzling juice. 'Is that all right?'

'What about the sausages?' I say.

'I ate those,' says Sid, handing me the tin. 'Watch out for the cherry stones. You were a long time. Everything all right?'

'Oh yes,' I say. 'Nice old couple. I've got to go and phone up and see if their cat is all right. Ridiculous, isn't it?'

'Keep the customer satisfied,' says Sid. 'The motto has stood us in good stead since our days as window cleaners.' He yawns. 'Don't be surprised if I'm asleep when you get back. This country air really takes it out of me. I've never known anything like it.'

'You sleeping in the pigsties?' I ask.

'*The ablutions*,' he says firmly. 'Yes, we can think about something more permanent tomorrow. What are you doing?'

'I don't know yet,' I say, staring at the battered pine-apple cubes in the bottom of the tin. 'At the moment it's a toss-up between starving to death and sleeping in the car.'

The only telephone box in the village is full of sugar beet so I end up phoning from The Three Jolly Rapists. You would think that on Friday night at carnival time the place would be doing some business but there is not a soul there. Even the landlord comes from next door in a dressing gown and looks surprised to see me. 'We don't serve a lot of people at this time of night,' he says accusingly when I ask for a packet of crisps and a pint of the local cider. I apologise and get another dirty look when I ask if I can use the telephone.

'Shouldn't think you'll still find Miss Blenkinsop at the exchange,' says the landlord grudgingly. 'She's not one to hang about – not since the Yanks pulled out, anyway. The vicar had to speak to her, you know. Mind you, I'm not one to point the finger. "Let him who is without sin cast the first stone." That's what I always say. Nobody's perfect and there was a war on. "Oversexed, overpayed and over here," that's what we used to say.'

'About Miss Blenkinsop?' I ask.

'No! About the Yanks.' The landlord looks at me contemptuously,

'Of course, you weren't alive then, were you?' He says it like I ought to feel guilty. Like I carefully arranged it so that I was not born until after World War II thus leaving him to fight Germany by himself with the help of a few thousand sex-mad Yanks who were having it off with Miss Blenkinsop. I expect he fancied her himself. Probably just on the point of popping the question when the first Liberator droned over the marshes.

We exchange a few more words neither of us wants and I get my hands on the telephone. Miss Blenkinsop, or someone, is there and I get through to Finchley Town Hall and leave a message for Mr Lucus. Being of a sensitive disposition I don't fancy talking to him myself. Just the sound of his voice would make Percy wilt guiltily. I would much rather leave him there happily trying to kick somebody's gunga din up their hooter.

I put down the phone and return to my cider. I don't know how strong it is but it tastes dry enough to kindle a fire in your belly. There are a lot of bits floating in it as well, and they are not all morsels of crisp. I hold it up to the light and it is like looking into a snowstorm.

'All right for your taste?' says the landlord sarcastically.

I assure him that it is a very interesting brew and slap down the necessary ackers on the counter. I don't want to leave Patty too long in case she reckons that I am not coming and turns in. I wish the landlord a hearty good night, take two steps towards the door and – blimey! My knees suddenly pack it in and I divebomb the floor as if performing a speeded up curtsey.

'You want to be careful of Old Mildew,' says the landlord. 'Most of the locals make a pint last an evening.'

I toss off a light laugh that comes out like Ken Dodd gargling with trifle and stagger outside. Surely it can't just be the drink? It must be the combined effect of my night on the beam and all that mine clearing and carpentry. I am not myself. Maybe I should give Patty a miss? On the other hand, Captain Mushkick will soon be flexing his triceps all over the greensward and my chance will have gone. After my disappointment with Dimity, can I inflict more deprivation on myself? I know the answer before I ask myself the question and take a few steadying breaths outside the door of the pub. The night is alive with the scent of horse manure, and whatever else you can say about the pong, it certainly sobers you up a treat. I am just driving past the village green when I hear a strangled cry for help. Walter Looney has been practising maypole dancing and has lashed himself to the pole. I cut him free and go on my way rejoicing. If you only save a fellow human being's life once a day it is still worth doing.

When I get back to the field Sid's fire has died down to a few embers and the most comforting glow is that which comes from the window of the Lucas caravan. I check that Sid is kipping and glide through the dewy grass with my senses tingling. Of course, I could be in line for no more than a cup of tea but somehow I don't think so. There was something in that bird's eyes that they never get round to in 'Swiss Family Robinson'. I know from experience with my own dearly beloved sister that women can go a bit funny after the birth of the first born. Just when you think they ought to be cooing over the woolly booties, they are planning one way trips to South America and laughing at the milkman's jokes. Home is a prison with the walls made of damp nappies and when they take baby for a walk they wheel him past the boating lake and find themselves wondering how deep it is. I reckon that Patty is going through that period and that she craves something more out of life than is likely to be offered by a caravan holiday at Little Crumbling. Being married to a karate fiend can't help – I mean, it doesn't exactly reek of sensitivity, does it. It's bad enough wanting to punch somebody up the throat – but trying to kick them in the goolies at the same time . . . no, it's not nice.

I run my fingers through my barnet, take a deep breath, shove my hand down the front of my trousers to flick percy into an action stations position and tap lightly on the caravan door.

'Yes. Who is it?' The voice sounds nervous.

'It's me, Patty. Timothy Lea. Everything all right?' I say the bird's name because it sounds friendly and breeds confidence. Also, it is flattering when people remember your name.

'Oh yes. Hang on a minute.' I hear her making exasperated noises as she struggles with the lock and then the door opens. The more optimistic side of my nature had hoped to find her wearing a diaphanous black nightie slung like a tight rope between her erect nipples but this is sadly not the case. She has on a woolly pullover and a pair of jeans. Still, they are both on the tight side.

'Come in,' she says. 'I just put the kettle on. Did you get through all right?'

'I left a message,' I say.

'Thanks so much. I was thinking after you left that I should have looked up some train times. Is it easy to get here by rail?'

I seem to remember passing Crumbling Junction and that the station building had been turned into a bungalow with a chicken run where the line used to be. This is probably not what Mrs Lucas wants to hear.

'I'm not certain,' I say. 'I don't expect he'll have too much trouble. That's a nice jumper.' Peacock blue is, I believe, the colour but it is the knockers that I am subjecting to the full force of my gaze.

'Oh these – I mean, this?' she says. 'Do you like it? I'm

not sure myself. I haven't thought about clothes for so long. Not with the baby and everything.'

'I would never have known that you had one,' I say. 'I mean, figurewise. My sister took a long time to get her figure back. She had to do exercises.'

'I think it depends what type you are. I never had to do anything.' We both stare at Patty's body like it is some kind of exhibit in a museum. 'You will have a cup of tea, won't you?'

'Oh yes,' I say cheerfully. 'That was what brought me round here.' Lying sod, Lea!

'Milk and sugar?'

'Ta. One spoonful, please.' I sit down on a bunk with my cuppa and look round the caravan. 'Where's Elgin, Playing with his marbles?'

I don't think she understands my archeological joke because she looks slightly puzzled. 'He's asleep,' she says, nodding towards the carrycot which I now recognise on the floor at the far end of the caravan. 'He's sleeping right through now.'

'That's handy,' I say. 'My sister's kids never did that. She had the first one when they were living with us and it used to scream all night.' And most of the day, I might add. I don't think there was ever a child like Jason Noggett for the full frontal assault on the eardrum. He was so bad that Dad used to go to work to get away from him.

'They can be difficult,' says Patty, sitting at the table and stirring her tea. 'I've been very lucky with Elgin.'

I nod and silence is resumed. It suddenly occurs to me that it may not be all right to have a go at her. Perhaps it is too early after the birth of the child. They must take a bit of time to get back to normal. I try and think back to Sid and Rosie. As far as I can remember, Sid began looking more relaxed the moment she got back from hospital.

Still, Sid lacks a lot of my sensitivity. I would hate to put my foot in it.

'I wonder how Malcolm's getting on?' says the bird.

'Yes,' I say. I don't want to talk about Malcolm but I don't seem to be able to jog the conversation into a new groove. It must be that pint of Old Mildew. I am nearly dropping off.

'It'll make such a difference to the holiday if he does well.'

I can just see it. Taking the kiddy down to the beach to practise kicking sand in people's faces. 'They didn't say anything when you rang?'

'Nothing.'

'He's probably still in, then.'

I should be so lucky, I think to myself. Wake up, Lea! Where is the old dazzling repartee that has made you the toast of the Balham Rotary Club Rejects' Sporting Association? 'How long are you planning to stay for?' I hear myself asking.

'Two weeks, I think, but it depends on Mal. He's so changeable. Footloose and fanny – I mean, fancy free.'

'Is he?' I say, lighting upon her slip of the tongue. 'I mean, does he fancy the birds?'

'Why should I talk to you about it?' she says.

'No reason at all if you don't want to,' I say. 'I was just interested, that's all. Where's he staying tonight?'

The bird shoots me what I believe is known as a quick glance, 'You're very nosy,' she says. 'At home, of course.'

'Oh,' I say.

'What does that mean?'

'Nothing. Just oh.'

'If you think he's got some tart round there, you can think again. He wouldn't dare! Not—' she breaks off and stares at me, eyes blazing.

'Not after the last time?' I say. Yes, Sherlock Lea has

struck again and you don't have to consult Watson (another sophisticated joke. Don't worry if you don't get it) to realise that I have hit upon the truth.

'I was carrying Elgin,' she says.

I suck in my breath through horrified Teds. Carving up the bints whilst your old lady is in the pudding club is not top drawer behaviour even down Scraggs Lane. 'I'm sorry,' I say. 'I wish I'd never touched upon it.' I accompany the word 'touched' with the friendly pressure of my hand on hers and smile understandingly into her eyes. It is a gesture that clearly disturbs her.

'I'd better go and see if Elgin is all right,' she says. She starts to get up but I refuse to let go of her hand. 'Don't go away,' I say. 'He's all right. You know he is.' She hesitates and then sits down again. 'You don't have to spend every moment of your life thinking about him,' I say. 'Not unless you want an excuse.'

'What do you mean, excuse?' she says.

'To stop you behaving how you'd like to behave. You're bottling it all in at the moment. You'd like to make love, wouldn't you?' I hope I sound confident because it is just a stab in the dark. She might feel like making a model of Westminster Abbey out of matchsticks. She looks at me and I see her eyes widen as if what I have just said has made her think about what I have just said. I don't hang about but swiftly get up and stand beside her so that I can put one hand on her shoulder and bend down next to her cheek. Still she does not say anything.

'Wouldn't you?' I repeat. I kiss the top of her ear through her hair and risk a crick in the neck pecking my way round to her north and south. I keep expecting her to say 'desist, Rodney! This is madness,' and give me a right hander round the chops but this little darling suddenly reveals herself as being full of pleasant surprises.

The moment my lips have brushed against her kisser

she grabs my nut like it has just shot out of the back of a rugby scrum and presses my cakehole against hers with enough force to dejuice a lemon. I hardly have time to coco what is going on before she has forced me back against the table. Is it my imagination or can I hear Kent Walton counting up to ten? If this is a sample of what she can do I reckon her old man must have been giving her lessons. I break free from her killer embrace for a second but she whips me back like she has plans to suffocate me with her knockers. What a way to go!

'Get those things off!' she barks. If I thought she was talking about clearing away the tea things she soon shows me otherwise by standing up and starting to peel off her jumper. Up it goes and a couple of cracking bristols bounce into view spilling out of a light blue bra. Faced with that kind of encouragement you can't just lie there, can you? I hurl myself into the ascendant – narrowly beaten by you know who – and start racing her down to the Y-fronts – though in her case the only slit in her pants is not in view. Not yet, anyway. She reaches behind her to unhook her bra and I slide my arms round her body and pinion her against my chest with my hands on hers. Her mouth comes up to mine and I ruckle her knockers against my chest and listen for the sound of the surf. Pity. The tide must be out – and not only the tide, ladies and gentlemen. Yes, fifteen and a half glorious metric centimetres of sturdy British tonk has lofted itself proudly into the air and is thrusting its ruby dome above the waistband of my underpants. Courage, England, all is not lost! This old country of ours is still second to none when it comes to turning out a nice quality hand produced article. Patty clearly likes the merchandise because her mit closes round its shaft as her mouth opens and her tongue pokes out through half parted lips. 'Bugger training!' she hisses and reapplies herself to my cakehole. The significance of this remark is initially lost on me but it dawns on me that it probably has something to do with hubby. She clearly has it in for him at the moment. And if him, why not—? I slide one hand into her panties round the back entrance and slip two and a half brace of digits in the front just in case anybody accuses me of giving short measure. Nothing seems to be amiss from what I can remember of my last saunter down Lovers' Lane and I feel that I can safely put my scruples behind me – on second thoughts, perhaps I will try something less acrobatic. I don't want to risk doing myself an injury just before the big feature.

'Come down on the floor,' pants Patty. 'We don't want anyone to see us.'

I had forgotten about that. It is odds on that old Walter Looney is poking about out there somewhere and a sight of our silhouettes in full fondle might be enough to drive him sane. I sink to the floor – I'll sink to anything given the right inducement – and find that Patty is already down there with time on her hands. She abandons time and returns to my hampton, pulling back my underpants so that he can jump another couple of inches towards the ceiling. 'Uhm,' she murmurs, running her fingers along him like she is stroking a dog she is not quite sure about. 'I haven't seen anything like this for a long time.'

'No karate chopper, eh?' I say, always one for a joke.

'Don't mention that word,' she says. 'I might bite it off.'

Such a thought is, to put it mildly, an unpleasant one and I am just about to remonstrate with her – it's all right. It is permissable between consenting adults – when the baby starts to make a noise. I had forgotten all about Elgin and his tiny whimper has a most unfortunate effect on my hampton. It is like when Alison Tonker's pet poodle started getting fruity when we were on the job together – I mean, me and Alison Tonker, of course. I would hate you to think that – but no, you couldn't, could you? I start feeling uncomfortable and my Mad Mick becomes a sad prick. I am not having it off with a woman any more but with a mummy. And mummies are different. The whole of little Elgin's future life might be affected by this incident. I read at the dentist that the early years are the important ones.

Patty is swift to spot my predicament – well, she is nearer to it than I am. 'It's all right,' she says. 'He's only stirring.' She giggles. 'Why don't you try it?'

'What, making that noise?' I say.

'No, silly! A bit of stirring. You've got the right instrument for it.' She looks down at percy and frowns. 'Or rather, you did have.'

'I'm worried about Elgin,' I say. 'It doesn't seem right with the kiddy down the end there.'

'I'm not putting him outside,' she says.

'I don't want you to,' I say. 'It worries me, that's all.'

'Lots of people do it when the baby's in the room. They have to. The babies don't mind. Elgin has to put up with his Dad trying to chop through half a dozen tiles. That's probably much more disturbing.'

'Yeah, I suppose you're right.'

'Listen, he's stopped now.'

'Yeah.'

'You're too sensitive.' She slips her fingers round my nob and starts polishing it with the pad of her thumb. 'Much too sensitive.' She trembles her lips and gazes down teasingly at the dome of my dick. I must say, what she is doing does concentrate the mind wonderfully. I don't seem to be half as worried about Elgin as I was a few moments ago. 'Who's a naughty boy, then?' With these words, her head goes down and a network of electric shocks fans up past my belly button. Half of them have set off even before her tingling tongue has dipped into the cleft of my purple war head and the rest belt after their mates when her warm

89

lips candle douse my hot tip and surround pampered percy with super sensational suction. Her cheeks hollow and she coaxes another half inch out of my giggle stick like she is trying to get a last drag out of a cigar butt. With this kind of cultured treatment, worries about wilting willy belong to the past. Lea's space probe has recovered all its old tensility and is quivering like a balloon in a strong wind. Loath as I am to put an end to such a delectable gobble there is only one place we can go from here and I feel that the occasion demands more of me. Old Mildew is still coursing round my veins and that, plus the delicious treatment being meted out to me at crutch level, stirs my amatory impulses – or makes me feel dead horny, putting it another way. With understandable tenderness I guide Patty's mush away from my glistening shaft and reward her for her endeavours with a long drawn out Swiss miss. At the same instant I wriggle sideways so that I can get my hands on her knicks and thrust them down towards her ankles. Once they are past her knees, I leave her mouth and rise up to pull off her panties and station myself between her legs. I draw them up so that they are resting against my chest and then lean forward pressing her back firmly against the carpet. Now, my shoulders slide down her calves and I pull open her legs and reveal her dilly pot nestling temptingly below me. I can trace its gleaming length through the fuzz like a jungle river seen from the air. I hold her glance for a second whilst we read each others minds – not recommended for those with high blood pressure – and slowly lower my nut. Her knees are pressed back against her knockers and the delicious furburger is thrown into tempting prominence. Choosing my spot with care, I arrow my tongue and shoot a few delicate dabs against the top of her clit slit. She starts to moan and I build up the strokes like a painter making sure that a difficult corner gets its full wack.

I must confess to being a bit of a nana when it comes to playing 'Spot the Clitoris' because it doesn't exactly stand out like Nelson's Column – not on most birds, anyway. Also, they respond in different ways when you touch it. Some go ape if you brush against it whilst with some birds you can lean against it like the bailiffs on a doorbell. I work on the principle of having a delicate feel around until the bint's reaction tells me that she likes what I am doing. Usually, this means gentle pressure beside the fairway and a spot of tweaking in the rough. This is purely digital, of course. With the brewer's bung I tend to start off as already described and then yo yo the whole length of the furry furrow occasionally plucking at its lips like a cat picking up its young. I also spread apart the goody with my fingers so that the nerve ends are brought nearer the surface and the delicate, darting motion of the tongue liberates more sensations. What is so pleasant about this is that it always – appropriately enough – goes down well. Half the pleasure of sex – perhaps more – is making someone else happy and when they are turned on then you feel twice as good and that makes one and a half times the pleasure you started off with – or maybe my maths is up the spout.

Anyway, I am glad to be able to report that Mrs Lucas is making me very happy indeed. Her eyes are closed and she is forming a lot of noises down at the back of her throat that you usually only hear in hotels with thin walls. My north and south is now in full swallow wallow and I am feeling as horny as a herd of wildebeest. One more light-ning lunge up and down the grand canal and I break off my minge munch, brush my lips against the inside of Patty's thighs and rise to the vertical. My hampton leaps into my hand like Billy the Kid's equaliser and I press its dimpled dome against the beauteous Berkeley. This is always my favourite disappearing trick. It beats rabbits any day of the week. Now you see it, now you don't. The purple headed bed snake glides slowly from view and I ease my weight forward and take my mouth down to Patty's. We kiss gently as percy measures his full length in the velvet void and I feel Patty's legs hooking over mine. She quivers from the top of her barnet to the tip of her these and those and a nervous ripple runs through my hampton. Space control had better get a grip or we will have blast off before we have lift off. I start to think about concrete Wellington boots and British Rail sandwiches and am relieved when the moment of danger passes. My fears about Patty's snatch were groundless. It is an amazing piece of work, the female grumble. It must stretch further than Britain's national debt.

'Go on,' says Patty. She slips her hands round my bum and urges me into her as if she hopes there might be another couple of inches held back for emergencies. I wish I could oblige but her only chance would be if I potted one of my bollocks up her snatch with the end of my dick and I haven't brought my chalk with me.

'Right!' I say. I slap my hands down on either side of her rocks and boulders and start stirring her dilly pot with a figure of eight motion. The penetration varies like the rise and fall on a Scalectrix track and as the rhythm builds up so does Patty's excited breathing. Her fingers dig into my flesh and it is obvious that her big moment is getting nearer with every cycle. I am not sorry because the fruit of the gonads can not much longer be kept in check. It has been a long hard day and my powers of restraint are not what they might be.

'Yes! Yes! Yes!' Patty's words stir me to a last vigorous stab at the furry doughnut and as she clings on to me like the last bus out of Cleethorpes, a delicious, liberating tidal wave of warmth sweeps through my loins. Oh! That was smashing. What a lovely way to go. And how much better for it is going to be my kip tonight. The thought of the shuteye to come is almost as pleasant as what has just passed. I only hope I have the strength to get back to the car. I tactfully smother a yawn and look round for my clobber.

'Don't bother,' says Patty, kissing me lightly on the cheek. 'I'll lock the door. We don't want anybody interrupting our night of love, do we?'

CHAPTER FIVE

In which Timmy comes to grips with nudism in the shapely forms of nicely born Sylvia Lestrange and swiftly aroused Cherry.

When I wake up the next morning I feel like my Gran's crab apple jelly – as if I have been strained through a sheet of muslin. I don't know what Patty was trying to get out of her system but she got more out of mine than I would have thought possible. When I open my mince pies it is as if the lids have been stuck together with fish glue and the lower part of my body is no more than a tender memory. I am lying on the floor with a blanket over me; the grey light coming through the window suggests that it is morning. I turn my head to left and right but there is no sign of Patty. I peer over my exposed toes and there she is, sitting by the stove breast-feeding Elgin. The little bleeder is sucking greedily and I can't help feeling embarrassed. I mean, me sucking a bird's titties is all right, but a baby, well, it's not quite nice, somehow.

'Morning,' she says cheerfully. 'I'm just giving Elgin his breakfast. Do you fancy some?' She reads my expression and sticks her tongue out at me. 'I mean, a cup of tea!'

'Great,' I say. 'What time is it?'

'Oh, about seven, I think.' She leans forward, still cradling the baby and glances towards the clock on one of the shelves. 'Oh my God!' She sees something out of the window that turns her face whiter than the milk in a baby's bottle.

'What is it?' I am rising like a rocket even before she has the chance to answer.

'It's Malcolm!' I press my mug to a corner of the window and peer round the curtain. He doesn't look like a Malcolm to me. More like a Mangler. His fists are thrust deep into the pockets of his overcoat and he is picking his way towards the caravan through a sea of mud. It must have rained again during the night. He has a black eye, a mean expression and the last time I saw a pair of shoulders like that they were being worn by a gorilla. He is about fifty yards away and in my present condition that is about five miles and fifty yards too near.

'Get out!' shrills Patty helpfully. 'He'll kill me.' Yeah, I think to myself. He'll probably beat you to death with my corpse. I look around for somewhere to hide but there is nowhere. 'Get out the back!' squeals Patty.

The door points away from the entrance to the site and she puts down the baby and wrenches it open so fast that it nearly says goodbye to the hinges. I reach out for my pants but she grabs my arm and hauls me to the entrance.

'There's no time to waste!'

I don't get around to arguing the toss with her because she shoves me down the steps and shuts the door in my face. Nice, isn't it? So much for romance. When the old man comes up the garden path, you are not the only thing that goes out of the window. I am now starkers and about twenty yards from the hedge which surrounds the nature reserve. I could make a bolt for it but the odds are that Malcolm would spot me – not so much spot me as scar me for life. Better not risk it. I take a deep breath and throw myself full length in the long grass. Ooh! What bleeding agony. Not only long grass but nettles as well. And cold. And wet! I find myself face to face with a large orange slug and close my eyes. Maybe it would be best if Patty's old man did see me. Then he could put me out of my agony. I crawl a few feet into the grass and wait. Elgin has started screaming and soon I hear the squelch of feet aproaching and a sharp rat-tat-tat on the door.

'Mal! What a surprise! Ooh, what's happened to your poor face? Did you win? Oh, what a shame.'

There is the sound of the door closing and I am left with a thistle sticking into my goolies and the memory of Patty Lucas's ability as an actress. They are dead cunning, women. There is no getting away from it. I wait a few more minutes until Elgin has belted up and Mr and Mrs Lucas seem engaged in normal domestic conversation and continue to wriggle towards the shelter of the hedge. Once I get behind it I will be able to skirt the field and get round to Sid's car. There are always a few pairs of birds knickers shoved down the back of the seats which will tide me over until I get back to the wash house. There is a lot of stretch in a pair of bird's knicks these days.

My Teds are chattering like a brace of castanets by the time I squeeze through a gap in the hedge and I don't think I have felt so uncomfortable since I watched Eric Morley at the last Miss World contest. I wonder where the nearest place is I can get a hot bath? London, I should think. I remove a bramble from my fife and slowly raise my freezing, aching limbs to the vertical. Beyond the hedge, the Lucas's caravan seems to be rocking on its moorings and I entertain the unwholesome suspicion that Mrs L is on the job again. Is there no containing the woman? After the night of unsurpassed ecstasy that she has extracted from my limbs I find it rather repulsive that she should be once more entertaining the rubiate prong. All that and feeding her baby too. The whole earth mother bit. It is not surprising that blokes develop complexes. I mean, they even live longer than us, don't they? Such deep and disturbing thoughts are sifting through my nut when I suddenly hear a twig snap behind me. Is it a heavy pheasant or – cringeville! A beautiful blonde piece of crackling is willowing through the undergrowth towards me. This would be remarkable enough even if the bird was not starkers. Yes, starkers! Identical in lack of clobber to myself. Without a stitch of clothing to call her own. What is happening? Maybe I have been watching too much black and white television through Dad's coloured slides. It can't be good for you, even without the programmes.

'Yew hew. Ripping, isn't it?' The bird is addressing me, like the sight of a naked geezer trying to hide his weasel behind a teasle comes as no surprise to her. 'Sylvia Lestrange. I don't think we've met. Did you come last night?

'Did you come last night?' What a question. More times than carol singers on the first of December. But how can she tell? And why is she starkers?

'I think this is the best time of the day, don't you? Before everybody gets up.'

'Before everybody gets up'. The words make me wince. I don't think I will ever get up again. 'It's all right,' I say, guardedly.

'Have you seen anything interesting in the flora and fauna line? I just caught a glimpse of the most beautiful tit.'

There must be an answer to that if I think long enough. This bird's top bollocks are definitely something to write home about if you have a broad-minded Mum. She looks better naked than most judies with half a whale round their knockers. More uplift than you get on BBC 2. Even in my present perished condition I can respond to a top drawer article when brought face to Manchester with one of them. But how did she know I had been having a trolley and truck? Must be the state of the old Marquis I suppose. It does look like a piece of string that has been towed behind an outboard motor.

'I can see you're new here,' she says nodding at my hands. 'You're hiding your parts. I've noticed lots of the chaps doing that. Actually, when you think about it, it just makes them more obvious. Much better to let them dangle.' What a funny woman. I wonder if she has escaped from anywhere. My Uncle Ron once gave a lift to a naked bird who was on the run from a nut farm. He said that she made the most incredible demands on him and that it was a good job that the police thought she was making it up when she told them what had happened. It was not as bad as it sounds because Uncle Ron was round the twist and half way back again. They were made for each other.

'I'm certain they're no different to anyone elses. Not very pretty but nothing to be ashamed of.' She reaches down and pulls my hand away. 'There, see? I would never notice it.'

'Thanks,' I say. 'Oh well, better be getting along, I suppose.'

I don't have time to humour her or the inclination to do anything else. Better get back to Sid and see if he has any aspirins. I am obviously going through one of my difficult periods.

'Don't you fancy a tramp across the dunes?' says Sylvia. 'Jolly bracing.'

'I'm frozen,' I say. 'I don't know how you can stand it out here.'

'Practise,' says Sylvia. 'You'll soon get the hang of it.' She gives my petrified hampton a funny look. 'We don't need all these togs, you know. We've conditioned ourselves to them. If we went naked all the time we'd soon adjust. Come on, give me your hand. If you're cold we can scamper through the beech leaves.'

She is definitely nutty as fruit cake this bird but I can't help taking a shine to her. I suppose some of it is the upper class bunny. I have always been partial to the kind of bint who would not use my Y-fronts to lay a trail for her beagles. She is also incredible in the looks department. Miles better than you would get if you stuck a couple of tits on Harold Wilson – or Margaret Thatcher, for that matter. Still I must be getting back. Sid will be wondering what has happened to me.

'Another time,' I say summoning up a sample of the old world charm that makes Reginald Bosanquet come over like Jack the Ripper with a brain tumour. 'I must be getting back.'

'All right, I'll come with you,' says Sylvia brightly. 'Perhaps some brekker would be a good idea. Have you got a nice room?'

At first, I think she has said 'have you got a nice womb?' it is probably a hangover from Patty – so it takes me a few moments to get my thoughts together. 'I haven't really got straightened out yet.' I say eventually. I glance down at my dick and it seems to have shrunk to the size of Elgin's little finger. It protrudes from my shrunken cluster like a wart on the side of a gooseberry. If it gets any smaller it will be inside me and the consequences of that are too unpleasant to think about. I wonder if you can go to prison for having it off with yourself? Depends if you were consenting, I suppose. While my restless mind is considering a decision that could make legal history, Sylvia has grabbed my mit and is pulling me after her impulsively.

'Come on!' she trills. 'Don't be a sad soak! We'll soon warm you up.'

The last part of the message gets through to me and for no other reason than that it might save my life I allow myself to be dragged down an avenue of trees carpeted with last autumn's leaves. Sylvia kicks them in the air with whoops of glee and I wait for white-coated men to appear and carry her away. At least it warms me up though the soles of my plates are going through agony.

'That was fun,' I gasp. 'But I think I'd better turn back now. I—'

'Oh super!' interrupts Sylvia. 'There's Mummy and

Daddy. I'll be able to introduce you. Yoo hoo! Mumsy!!'
I follow her waving mit and nearly have a heart attack.
A middle-aged geezer and geezeress are ambling towards
us down a side path and they are both starkers.

'Hello m'dear,' says the bloke taking a pipe from his
mouth. 'What have you been up to, 'eh?'

'Just having an early morning nature ramble, Dadsy. I
bumped into a fellow spirit.'

They all look at me and I stand there with my hands
over the place where my goolies used to be and wonder
whether I might be able to disappear into the ground if I
scrabbled my feet backwards and forwards very fast.
Sylvia's mum must be about fifty if she is a hundred and
five and I have never seen a woman of that age naked –
correction: there was a terrible moment when the towel
that Dad was holding round Mum at Southend fell down
– he was pissed, naturally. That was the moment I decided to leave home. I mean, seeing your own Mum naked.
How indecent can you get? It gives me goose pimples
just thinking about it. Anyway, Sylvia's mum is not re-
acting like my Mum. She is just standing there very com-
posed and upper crust.

'Hermione Lestrange," she says, holding out a hand.
'How do you do?'

I dice with which hand to remove from my cluster and
find myself giving a sort of nervous curtsey. 'Timothy
Lea,' I say, squeezing her fingers. 'Pleased to make you –
I mean, meet your acquaintance – I mean, make your
acquaintance.'

Sylvia's mum's eyes narrow but she does not lose control of her stiff upper lip. 'And this is my husband, Edgar.'

Edgar takes his pipe out of his mouth again and shakes
my hand. It is funny but it is shaped exactly like his dick –
I mean, his pipe is. It curves out and then drops down.
It is big, too. Very big. Not what you would expect if you

saw Mr Lestrange with his clothes. It just goes to show. Nature is very indiscriminate with her gifts – good word that, isn't it? Indiscriminate. I just bunged it in for those of you who have been set this book for your 'O' levels.

'How d'you do, young man?' says Edgar. 'You look a bit chilly. You have to watch spring about here. It can be a bit treacherous.'

While he is talking about watch springs I am trying to take my eyes of Mrs Lestrange's knockers. I have not seen anything like them since we tossed a couple of kids in a blanket when I was at school. Only her belly sags lower and further than her enormous breasts. From a distance she looks like a melting pawnbroker's sign.

'Do watch that pipe, Edgar,' 'she snaps. Her old man has just tapped it against a tree and a shower of sparks have menaced her upholstery.

'Sorry, old gal,' he says. 'Righty ho. Time for brekker, what? You'll join us won't you, Mr Lea?'

I am now so cold and hungry that I will eat anywhere. Even in a lunatic asylum. 'Thanks very much,' I say.

'Is it your first time here?' inquires Mrs Lestrange as we stride down the avenue.

'That's right,' I say.

'The place needs some new blood,' says Edgar. 'One gets fed up with seeing the same old faces.'

'Not just the faces,' I say, with a light laugh.

'Er – quite,' says Edgar and I have the uncomfortable feeling that my little joke has not gone down well. Still, what is one more uncomfortable feeling after all I have been through?

Ahead of us the outline of a red brick mansion shows through the trees and I am surprisd to see that there are no bars on the windows. No wonder the inmates are wandering all over the grounds. It must have been them I saw on the beach and on the cliffs. It is a shame about Sylvia but at least she is with her mum and dad. It must make a difference if the whole family is round the twist.

The building hoves into view and – by the cringe! There are half a dozen naked bods playing crocquet on the lawn. I glance towards a peeling signboard poking out of the shrubbery and suddenly it comes to me – like the squitters after eating a couple of pounds of unripe apples. 'Little Crumbling Naturists' Sanctuary' – naturists not naturalists! The place is a nudist colony not a bird sanctuary.

'Oh fantastic!' I say. 'You're not barmy after all.'

Sylvia looks at me, puzzled. 'What do you mean?' she says.

'You're a nudist,' I say.

'Of course I am,' she says. 'So are you – aren't you?'

'Who, me?' I say. 'Oh yes – er, definitely. Love it. Back to nature, front to nature. Nature all over.' I see Mrs Lestrange looking at her husband and I lengthen my stride towards the house. I wonder how Sid will react to the news? Slap bang next to a nudist colony. What effect will it have on business? How would you like your little kiddy to clock Mrs Lestrange's breastworks over the ramparts of its sandcastle? It could do permanent damage.

We go through the front door and there is a large room on the right with a queue of people helping themselves to cornflakes and porridge. Porridge! I never used to like the stuff but in my present condition I could eat the lumps with a knife and fork.

'They've still got those damn wickerwork chairs, I see,' says Edgar indignantly. 'I don't want my BTM turned into a relief map of North Wales.'

'Edgar, please!' Mrs Lestrange sounds shocked. 'You're on the management committee. It's up to you to do something about it.'

'And the croquet balls, Daddy,' says Sylvia. 'They've got big chunks out of them.'

I press forward into the queue and – 'Ooops! Sorry.'
I have pressed forward a bit too hard. You have to be careful when you are only wearing your birthday suit. Most of
the people around me are on the elderly side but the bird
behind the counter dishing out the porridge is cute and
curvy. She gives me a quick up and down and I am not
certain whether she is checking out the equipment or
seeing if she can recognise me. She has tight black curls
– and her hairdo is nice as well.

'Porridge or sugar puffs?' she says.

'Porridge please,' I say. 'Ta.' I hold out a plate, lick
my lips and her eyes widen. Her own lips gleam is if they
have been polished and they swell invitingly like she has
been blowing a piece of fluff away from her hooter all
night. Some birds have wicked lips and this little Pall
Mall could be picked up on suspicion of giving dirty kisses
any day of the week and twice on Sundays. Even in my
present sorry state percy registers a quiver of interest and
brushes against the tablecloth. Oh dear this nudity lark is
so embarrassing. If the central heating was a mite warmer
percy might start – oh dear, why did I have to think of
that? The moment the thought enters my down the drain
I feel something stirring in the furrry thicket. You know
what it's like, lads. You dare not look but you know it is
happening. What a time and a place to choose. My hampton has no sense of decorum. One second a refugee from
the petrified forest, the next shooting up like a pantomime
bean stalk when the assistant stage manager has been on
the meths. I accidentally brush against the old bag in
front of me and she leaps forward as if I have dug a hypo-
dermic syringe into her bum. She whips round, glances
down, and her eyes close momentarily in horrified shock.

'Really!' she hisses. She picks up a fork and plunges it
into a bulging banger like she is bayoneting it. She should
be the kiss of death for percy but the foolish organ res-

ponds to the leathery withers as if serving as a prop in the Nigerian heat of the Miss Blow Job contest. Suddenly, he is bursting with rude vigour – and I mean rude. I bend my knees and try and shuffle along so that the naughty bit is below the table but it is not easy. I know it is my imagination but everybody seems to be looking at me. Control, Lea! Think of the bottom of Mary Whitehouse's handbag, a mountain of perished elastic bands, Bradford Town Hall made of cold chips – 'Sausage?' 'Ta, very much.' 'Fried bread?' 'Lovely.' My plate is soon groaning with goodies and my tongue is hanging down so far it nearly hides my embarrassment. 'Help yourself to tea from the urn.' 'Ta.' Phew! A quick cup of Rosie and I will be able to scarper to a corner and swap polite rabbit with the Lestranges whilst percy comes to terms with himself. I step up to the urn and – 'YAAAAAARGH!!' My nob brushes against the hot metal and my plate of nosh soars into the air. Before it hits the deck my hands are round my aggrieved hampton and every eye in the place is on me. Talk about embarrassing. I have never known anything like it.

'What happened? says Sylvia. 'They didn't leave the hot plate out again, did they? Here, you can have my pat of butter if you like.'

I don't answer because I am too busy groaning and it is the bird with the glistening chops and the coal black minge fringe who comes over all help and efficiency. 'If you pick up the bits, I'll take him to the first aid room,' she says.

'It's still in one piece,' I say.

'I was talking about the plate,' she says. 'Come round behind the counter. I've handled bigger problems.'

I am not certain I like the way she says that but I am grateful to escape from all the staring mince pies. 'Jolly bad luck,' says Sylvia. 'See you later.'

I give her a brave smile and follow Lotus Lips through the door behind the counter. The first thing I see is a bacon slicer but I try not to think about it. I suppose you get used to be being starkers after a while. I certainly hope so.

'I'm Cherry, by the way,' says the bird. 'Come into my den and let's check out the damage.'

She leads me through another door and I find myself in a neatly furnished little office. If I was going to be honest I would have to admit that the couch is the first thing that catches my eye. Cherry closes the door and puts an accusing finger on my chest. 'OK. Level with me.'

'You mean, get on the couch?'

'That as well. What are you doing here? You're not one of our members if you'll excuse the expression.'

I scramble on to the couch because I reckon I look more helpless lying down and make a few 'Oo! Ah!' noises as the cold plastic gets to grips with my skin. 'No,' I say. 'It's all been an unfortunate misunderstanding really. I don't quite know how to put it.' We both look down at my crumpled Marquis of Lorne and I switch my gaze to the medicine cabinet on the wall.

'You're not the first,' says Cherry. 'We've had people like you before. The vicar of Twittlingfield Parva was in here one day saying that he had caught his cassock on a briar.'

'Are you suggesting that I'm a Teeping Pom?!' I say, indignantly. 'I mean, a Peeping Tom!' I would utterly repudiate that suggestion if I knew what repudiate meant.

'Some of our members are not much better,' says Cherry. 'I'm constantly having to check over their bona fides.' She glances back to my goolies and I think what a full rich life she must lead. 'They're more interested in each other's bodies than in the open air life.'

'How very unpleasant,' I say. 'I'm not at all like that. I

didn't even know this place was a nudist camp when I came in here.'

Cherry laughs scornfully. 'I wish I had a pound for every time I've heard that. I suppose you lost your clothes in a combine harvester? That's the most normal excuse.'

'You surprise me,' I say. 'Look, if you can lend me a pair of swimming trunks I'll be on my way and spare you further bother. I'll post them back to you.'

Before she can comment on my suggestion the door opens and a harassed looking geezer in specs shoves his head round it. 'What's the trouble?' he asks, nodding at me.

'Scorched penis,' says the bird – just like that.

'That blasted urn, I suppose,' says the bloke. 'At least it's not as bad as what happened with Mrs Hargreaves.'

'What did happen with Mrs Hargreaves?' I say, hating myself for asking.

'Poor old girl was a bit short-sighted. She mistook some chap's apparatus for the spout of the urn and twisted what she thought was the handle forty-five degrees to the right. I believe he's just come out of the special care unit.' I close my eyes. Why did I have to ask? 'Pop up and see me when you've finished, Miss Balsam. There's a few things I want to talk to you about.'

'That's Mr Friar,' says Cherry as the door closes. 'He's the warden, poor man.'

'What's the trouble?' I say, always sympathetic in the presence of a bird with such stand-out top bolics.

Cherry sighs. 'Mr Friar is a great nudist but a poor administrator. The two often go hand in hand.'

'Well, you've got nowhere to stick your biros, have you?' I say understandingly.

'I don't know where he'd be if he didn't have me as a general factotum,' muses Cherry.

I can't think of an answer to that one so I go back to

staring at the medicine cabinet. Cherry follows my gaze and nods briskly.

'Better do something about your problem, hadn't I? I'll look for some trunks in a minute.'

'I think it's all right now,' I say.

'Not sensitive?' Cherry holds my glance and slowly opens the door of the medicine cabinet. 'We'd better not take any chances.' She rummages along the shelves and comes back to the couch holding a small tube. 'Medicine cabinets are such a mess, aren't they? All those things you should have thrown away.' She sits down on the edge of the couch and unscrews the top of the tube. 'Are you sure you're not one of the thrill seekers?' She squeezes a small dab of transparent ointment on to the top of her erect index finger and gazes into my eyes.

'What are you going to do?' I ask.

'I think you are,' says Cherry. 'You can always tell. They're the excitable ones. The ones who can't control themselves.' She starts flexing her finger and I will swear that percy starts twitching in time with her digit.

'What is that stuff?' I ask, nodding at the ointment. It is melting on the tip of her finger and the shape is changing as it starts to run down towards her palm.

'They're very easily stimulated by what is happening about them.' She runs her tongue along her glistening lips and I suddenly think how nice it would be to find that someone had nudged your cakehole against them. Percy changes his position like a garden hose uncurling in strong sunlight and the throbbing sensation is not only caused by his brush with the urn.

'Dirty men,' continues Cherry as if she is not totally disgusted by the thought. 'Men who like to look because they're frightened to touch.' Her lips swell as if they are being pumped up like two small lilos and I suddenly realise that I would like to eat them. They remind me of a couple of bits of underdone liver – the only thing my Mum underdoes well – and in my present state of starvation I could have a go at anything. Those knockers, for instance – cor! Like a couple of milk puddings topped with figs.

'Men who like to be touched, long to be touched.' Cherry does not take her mince pies off me but her left hand – the one with the ointment on it – drops between my legs. I close them together automatically, and trap her fingers. 'Relax!' Her voice retains its gentle, silky quality and her slippery finger swiftly makes contact with the tip of my Mad Mick. There seems to be more to make contact with every second and I take a few moments off to marvel at the heroic stupidity of my starving stab stalk. Where does he find the strength from? It can't be me. I am knackered.

'You don't have anything to eat in that cupboard, do you?' I ask.

Cherry smiles at me whimsically and runs her free hand through my tousled hair. 'You're a strange boy,' she says. 'You're trying to sublimate, aren't you?'

'I don't think so,' I say. 'I think I'm trying to get something to eat before I snuff it.'

'Snuff it,' says Cherry. 'There you go again. All right, I'll snuff out your candle.' And, so help me, she bends down and starts giving me the kiss of life. All very nice but what I really want is a bacon sandwich. Honestly, sometimes I despair of birds. You can get more sensitivity out of a french letter made from a knotted inner tube.

'Look,' I say. 'Please—!'

'Lie back, you animal!' My shoulder blades hit the plastic like they have been fired out of a catapult and Cherry follows her thrust by leaping astride my thighs and grabbing my hampton like she intends to crack me over the nut with it. 'Don't fake it,' she growls. 'This is what you came for, isn't it?'

'Only if you haven't got a Mars bar,' I say. 'Look, I don't think you quite understand. I want—'

'I know what you want!' Wap! That was my cock making contact with the back of her snatch. She bungs it in so hard that I am amazed it does not bounce straight out again.

'No!' I bawl. 'You've got it all wrong. What I really want is something to e-e-e-e-e-e-' She is shuddering up and down on me like a groundsheet in a gale and I have a distant feeling that something is happening where I used to have balls. It is not so much a sensation as a parched croaking noise. The spasm passes and I readdress myself to my problem. 'Eat!' I gasp. 'That's what I want to do. I've got to eat something.'

'Lover!' A strange light flares up in Cherry's glazed eyes. 'Why didn't you say!?' She deserts the remains of my cluster and charges up my body.

'No!' I shriek wildly as the ultimate pair of glistening lips shudder before my cakehole. 'I didn't mean tha-ffleugugh!!!' Oh well, you can't win them all.

CHAPTER SIX

In which Timmy becomes involved in a merger and a novel form of blind man's buff is played in a woodland glade.

'Where have you been?' says Sid. 'Do you know what time it is? Well? Answer me! It's half past eleven and that's the ninth piece of sliced bread you've noshed in thirty-five seconds. That was supposed to last till the end of the week. Do you know how much bread costs these days?'

'Sorry, Sid,' I say.

Sid removes a piece of soggy bread from the corner of his eye and tries to hurl it at the floor. It sticks to his finger. 'Sorry? You bleeding ought to be sorry and all! You stand there in a pair of tart's knickers having left me to finish off the shit-house and all you can say is sorry Sid. You know I had to spend all last night on the roof, don't you?'

'No Sid! What was the trouble?'

'That bloody pig came round and tried to get into bed with me. When it found I wasn't you, it pulled all the blankets off and bit me in the ankle.'

'Oh dear,' I say. 'That's not very nice. By the way, did you know there was a nudist's camp next door? A bloke there made me a very interesting proposition.'

'I'm not surprised,' says Sid. 'In those drawers I might be tempted myself.'

'No Sid,' I say – because you have to show patience with him. 'His name's Friar. He runs the place. When I told him about our operation he was very interested.'

'But we haven't had an operation,' says Sid. 'What did you tell him we were – Siamese twins?'

'Ho, ho, Sid,' I say. 'Contagiously whimsical. No, I told him about the caravan site. At first he wasn't very thrilled but then he began to warm to the idea.'

'Wait a minute,' says Sid. 'Are you telling me that you have been inside this nudist camp?'

'Well,' I say. 'In a manner of speaking—'

'In the buff?'

'Er – yes, Sid.'

'Then these must be yours.' Sid nods towards a pile of these and those.

'Oh yes,' I say. 'Where did you find them?'

'Scattered round where our first client was parked,' says Sid grimly. I look across the field and see that the Lucas's caravan has indeed disappeared. Two muddy ruts make a straight line for the entrance as if it left at speed. 'Didn't even stop to say good morning,' says Sid. 'I stepped forward to claim our dues and copped a faceful of mud for my trouble. I had to change my trousers.'

'How unfortunate,' I say. 'I wonder what got into them?'

'I know what got into her!' says Sid through gritted teeth. 'You did, you horny little bastard! That's why they pulled out in such a hurry – I wish to God you'd done the same thing.'

'Sid,' I say. 'You've no grounds for saying—'

'Let me make one thing quite clear,' says Sid wearily. 'This is not going to be a knocking shop. You keep your cock under control or I'll confiscate it. For one thing, I've telegrammed Rosie and the kids to come down, and for another, gutter lust has no place in the scheme of things at "Noggett Super Hols". This isn't the Club Mediteranna-a-a-a, you know. We work on a more ethereal plane here. It's enrichment of the mind and spirit, communion with nature, all the aspects of my complex personality that I'v been seeking to express for so many years.'

'Sounds wonderful, Sid,' I say. 'Well, I think you and Mr Friar could have a very meaningful discussion. You seem to speak the same language.'

'That's always handy,' says Sid. 'I don't like dealing with foreigners.'

Half an hour later we are approaching the front entrance to the Naturists' Sanctuary. There is a metal gate barring the way and a bloke in a peaked cap comes out of the little cottage as we ring the bell.

'Good morning, my good man,' says Sid. 'I am Sidney Noggett, Chairman and Managing Director of Noggett Super Hols and my personal assistant here has arranged an appointment with your Mr Friar.'

'You come from the field next door, don't you?' says the man, not unkindly. 'Come in. You can change in the lodge.'

'Change?' says Sid.

'Undress,' says the gatekeeper. 'You don't want to offend anybody.'

'But you've got a uniform on,' says Sid.

'Only the front part of me,' says the man. 'The bit that faces the road.'

'Blimey!' says Sid. We walk behind the bloke and he is quite right. He is only wearing half a uniform. From his neck to his bum and down to his ankles he is stark fife naked at the back.

'How blooming stupid,' says Sid as we struggle out of our clothes. 'He can never turn round, that bloke. He has to shuffle backwards and forwards like a chess man.'

'Don't stand with your hands like that,' I say. 'It tells everybody you're a new boy. Let it all hang out. No need to tug it either.'

'It was a bit cramped,' says Sid. 'I'm not ashamed of it.'

'Of course you're not,' I say. 'Anyway, they say that size doesn't make any difference.'

'What's that supposed to mean?' says Sid. 'Are you suggesting that I've got a small one? It's as big as yours any day of the week!'

'Of course it is, Sid,' I say, soothingly. 'No need to get your knickers in a twist. I'm certain it's very serviceable.'

'Don't patronise me!' says Sid. 'We'll measure them. That's the only way to settle this.'

'Don't be stupid, Sid. I wasn't trying to start anything. We'll say yours is bigger if you like.'

'Oh no we won't! We'll prove it,' says Sid. 'You're not wriggling out now. I know you. Later on you'll be saying that because we didn't measure it, it doesn't prove anything.'

'I won't, Sid,' I try and reassure him. 'Honest, I won't.'

'I don't suppose you've got a tape measure,' says Sid. 'You wouldn't have, would you? It's one thing going around sneering at the size of other people's cocks but when it comes to the test, you're chicken!' He picks up one of his shoes. 'We'll use this bootlace. Hold it against the cock and tie a knot in it.'

'That's going to be rather uncomfortable, isn't it?' I say.

'Tie a knot in the piece of string!' says Sid. 'Gordon Bennett. You can be thick sometimes.'

'I don't see the point of this exercise,' I say. 'I mean, it's size now – in repose, so to speak – doesn't bear any relation to the moment of truth, does it?'

'What are you suggesting we do?' asks Sid. 'Start having a joddrell, or something?'

'I'm suggesting we forget the whole thing,' I say. 'It's not going to prove anything.'

'No-oh!' Sid pulls out his boot lace and flicks himself viciously in the balls. I try not to laugh. 'You're not going to be able to duck out of it like that. The ratio of expansion must be about the same. Now—' he holds one end of the boot lace against the point where his hampton disappears into his fuzz and stares down his body '– that's about fair, I reckon. OK with you?'

'Ah-hem, Sid!' I say, raising my voice slightly. The gatekeeper has just come into the room and is staring at Sid in puzzled fashion.

'Down to here,' says Sid, moving his right hand along the string. 'I'm allowing a little extra to make up for the bend.'

'If you gentlemen are ready.' Sid snaps upright and turns the colour of a freshly painted post-box. 'You can leave your bootlace here, sir. It will come to no harm.' The gatekeeper steps to one side and gestures us towards the door.

'You might have told me he was there!' hisses Sid as we pass through. 'You're just trying to make a fool of me, aren't you?'

'You beat me to it every time,' I tell him.

The gatekeeper backs out of the door after us and jerks his finger over his shoulder. 'Straight up the drive. You can't miss it.'

'What did this bloke Friar have in mind?' says Sid as we pick our way past banks of daffodils.

'He didn't say anything pacific,' I say demonstrating my easy fluency with impressive dicky birds. 'But reading between the lines under his eyes, I reckon that the place is in a bad way and that he could be interested in some kind of merger.'

'Capital!' says Sid. 'I've seen enough to realise that this dump needs my experienced hand on the helm. That geezer on the gate for instance – diabolical! The GPO is run better.'

'Most of the people around here seem to be pretty old,'

I say. 'There's a few families but not much young blood.'

'It's your pop festivals,' says Sid. 'That's the trouble. They can run around naked all day so why should they pay for the privilege? I think we'll have to restructure the whole concept.' He looks down his body. 'You know this thing is an extension of all my dreams.'

'You mean your cock?' I say. 'Don't tell me we're back to that again!'

'The philosophy behind nudism, you berk!' says Sid. 'It's right back to the natural existence I've been rabbiting about. Throw off your clothes and live! That's why it's called naturism – see?'

'You ought to be on the telly, Sid,' I say. 'You make it all sound so easy. Like Kenneth Clark.'

'I've never fancied driving racing cars,' says Sid. 'It would be a ridiculous waste of this human flame called genius if I put myself in a position of risk. I'm better off placing my mind at the disposal of humanity.'

'They should dispose of it pretty quickly,' I say. 'Tell me, Sid. What line are you going to take with this Friar geezer?'

'I'm going to play it by ear,' says Sid 'Ooh! What a bloody stupid place to put a sprinkler.'

'You have to keep your eyes open round here,' I say.

Sid stops dusting water off his dick and gazes thoughtfully across the lawns. 'Ye-es,' he says. 'I see what you mean. What a cracking looking bird – I mean, what a classic example of everything we should stand for.'

'I know, Sid,' I say. 'I nearly get a hard on every time I look at her. That's Sylvia Lestrange.'

'I didn't mean that kind of stand!' scolds Sid. 'I mean, she represents what we should all be aiming for – physically. Come on, I intend to introduce myself.'

'Don't let on that I'm with you, Sid,' I say. 'She thinks I'm one of them.'

'I'm not surprised with those knicks you were wearing,' says Sid. He steps on to the lawn but is brought up short by a shrill cry from the french windows – it is about the only upbringing Sid has ever had.

'That's Mr Friar,' I say. 'Come on, we'd better get over there. You can chat up Sylvia later.'

'Chat up!' exclaims Sid. 'Chat up? My interest in that girl is purely professional. Her physical appearance means nothing to me. Is that clear?'

'Absolutely,' I say. 'Don't get your bread and lard caught in the french windows.'

Sid looks down and blushes. 'I'll stand behind you,' he says.

'No you won't!' I tell him. 'I don't want anybody getting the wrong idea about our relationship.'

'Good morning, gentlemen,' says Friar stepping forward to greet us. 'Are you feeling better now, Mr Lea? Miss Balsam tells me she was quite worried about you.'

I am not surprised. She could have had a manslaughter charge on her hands – or a rather more private place. What a way to go – muffed to death. Thank God Friar came in again when he did. Though how he could have believed she was giving me artificial respiration I will never know.

'Come into my private sanctum. Pleasant view, don't you think? – Out of the window. Take a seat. I'd be careful of that armchair if I were you.' Sid starts to rise and there is a loud 'swalch!' noise. 'It is a bit sticky, isn't it? I must get it covered. Now, your partner tells me that you're planning to run a caravan site next door to us. I'm not quite certain how that's going to affect our operation.'

'Could do it the world of good, squire,' says Sid briskly. 'Let's be quite open with each other. Let's not conceal anything.'

Friar stretches out his foot underneath his desk and his naked toe collides with Sid's ankle. Both men jump as if electrocuted and Friar cracks his instep painfully on the underside of his desk. Sid grimaces and continues.

'From what I can make out, things aren't so hot here. You're not running at capacity. You could do with a lot more naked botties frisking over the sward.'

Friar blinks. 'Well – er, certainly membership does seem to be down on last year.'

'And you're not pulling in the youngsters,' says Sid. 'On my way up here I only saw one cracking bi – one young person.'

'I've had grandmothers here,' says Friar.

'Your sex life is your own affair,' says Sid. 'What you get up to in your spare time is your business. I realise that there must be temptations. All I'm saying is that you have a problem and that I'm prepared to put my know how and experience at your disposal – for a consideration, of course.'

'You're a plain speaking man. Mr Nuthead,' says Friar.

'Noggett,' says Sid. 'Yes, I don't mince words. You can't afford to in my line of business. Time is money and the devil takes the hind legs.'

Friar, who must be mad, looks impressed. 'I like the cut of your jib, sir,' he says. 'What precisely did you have in mind?'

'We pool our resources,' says Sid. 'A caravan holiday with Noggett Super Hols automatically entitles you to enter The Wonderful World Of Nudism – for an extra charge, of course.'

'The Wonderful World Of Nudism?' muses Friar.

'That's you,' says Sid. 'We've got to put some zing and sparkle into the concept. Make it sound exciting and modern. Nobody knows what a naturist is and to a lot of people it sounds kinky. Let's not beat about the bush, let's come right out with it – we're nudists!' Sid bangs his fist on the desk and a bowl of pins and paper clips drops into his lap. There is a short but painful interlude whilst they are removed.

'I see,' says Friar. 'Perhaps we have become rather out of touch. Would your caravaners be nudists?'

'Not while they were on the site,' says Sid. 'We don't have enough cover from the beet processing plant. Anyway, that's part of the plan. I think there's a lot of people who wouldn't mind having a go at nudism but they're put off by all the palava – having to join a club and have their credentials scrutinised – that kind of thing. If they could just give it a try and see if they liked it – one afternoon, say – then they'd be in like a flash. Having the camp just next to the site makes it dead simple. There's also the ones who'll want to tell their friends that they've been to a nudist camp. We can get some special postcards printed – very discreet, of course. And car stickers. You know that one that says "We've visited the lions of Longleat"? Well, we can have "We've visited the loins of Little Crumbling".'

I have to confess that sometimes Sid can turn it on. He has even got me nodding my head in agreement.

'It all sounds very – er dynamic – is that the word?' says Friar. 'But what about the undesirable elements?' For some reason he looks at me. 'Surely there'll be people who just come along to gawp?'

Sid nods his head emphatically as if he expected the question and has already dealt with it. 'At the prices I propose charging we'll be glad of them,' he says. 'Don't get me wrong. I'm not trying to be cynical or money-grabbing. We all believe in the ideals of naturism. What does it matter if these ideals are subsidised by those who don't believe in them? Isn't there in fact a kind of justice in this? Those with purity of spirit can soar above the leering multitude.'

Friar brushes away a tear and I look out of the window

for the fork of lightning that is going to turn Sid into a split personality. Surprisingly, nothing happens.

'Wonderful, stirring words,' says Friar with a choke in his voice. 'I feel it must have been divine providence that sent you here.'

'Ta,' says Sid. 'You're probably right.'

'There's only one thing that needs to be resolved,' says Friar. 'The beach. We'll have to have segregation of course.'

'I don't know,' says Sid. 'What's the difference between a black bird and a white bird? Bigger knockers, I suppose—'

'Mr Friar means between the naked and the clothed,' I say, glad to be able to get a word in. 'By the way, we've – well, it was me really – I've mineswept the beach.'

After the way Friar has lapped up Sid I am looking forward to a little praise but the warden merely looks puzzled. 'Mines?' he says. 'The last mine was lifted in nineteen-fifty.'

'Come, come,' says Sid. 'My young assistant and I were privy to a large bang shortly after the last cliff fall. Walter Looney said—'

'Don't believe anything that terrible old man tells you,' says Friar. 'He's like all the people round here. Quite unreliable. The bang was probably caused by one of the cattle scarers that fell over the cliff in the fall.'

'You mean,' I say, 'I pushed that bleeding wheel-barrow—'

'Wonderful exercise,' says Sid. 'I've never seen your pectorals in better condition – in fact, I've never seen your pectorals before!'

'Look,' says Friar. 'The sun is coming out. Let us hope it is an omen. May the sun shine down on our corporate endeavours.' He stands up and scratches his dick. 'I expect you'd like to get the lay of the land, Mr Noggett. I'll ring for Miss Balsam. She'll be able to fill you in better than I would.'

'Definitely,' I say. Sid and Friar look at me and I smile pleasantly. 'I'll take a turn round the grounds if that's all right with Mr Friar,' I say. 'See you back at the site, Sid.'

I open the door and there is Cherry. Her eyes flash fire and her lips go into an Ali shuffle as she sees me. 'Animal!' she hisses. She tosses her head in the air and catches it neatly on her shoulders before brushing past me and entering the room – and when I say brush, I mean brush. You get a gentler action in a five minute car wash. I glance down and her strawberry ripples have put a horizontal parting in the hairs on my chest. Thank goodness that I am getting used to life in a nudist camp and that this kind of thing does not affect my – oh dear. I step hurriedly into the nearest doorway and prepare for things to go back to normal. How could percy be such a nana? I was not even thinking about a Friar Tuck and yet he is now lunging forward like a spade in a bus queue. Will the foolish instrument of ecstasy never learn? I am glancing nervously over my shoulder when I hear the door opening Eek! I whip round and there is Sylvia gazing down at my horrible handful.

'Is this a stick up?' she says gaily. 'What *are* you doing Timothy? Thank goodness it wasn't Mummy.'

'Nothing,' I wince. 'I'm sorry, I don't know what it is. I ate a lot of bread this morning. Maybe it's the self-raising flour.'

'Don't be embarrassed,' says Sylvia. 'I know it can be difficult sometimes. Even Daddy has problems. He was stung by a bee once. It wouldn't go away.'

'The bee?' I say.

'No, his thing!' says Sylvia. 'That's where it stung him. They had to pack it in ice.' I don't know if she intends it but something about Sylvia's story has a very diminishing effect on percy. He is in mid wilt even before she gets to the ice pack. 'Ah, that's better,' she says surveying the disappearing dongler. 'You know your trouble: you're too sensitive. You're too aware of your body. It's the body within nature that's important.'

'I suppose you're right,' I say.

'You daren't even look at me,' accuses Sylvia. 'Come on! You've got to come to terms with it sooner or later. I'm only a woman. I have hair and breasts and legs.'

'I know, but you have more of them than other women,' I say. 'I can't help finding you attractive. And when I find you attractive—' something tells me that I ought to pretend to look at the noticeboard.

'Oh dear,' says Sylvia. 'I see what you mean. Still, don't despair. I'm going to take you in hand.'

'Here?' I say.

'No, silly! In the garden.' Sylvia seizes me by the mit and whisks me towards the nearest french windows. 'I know what you need.'

'Are you sure?' I say, wishing I had finished off the rest of Sid's sliced loaf.

'Yes,' she says. 'We have a game here – well, it's a sort of therapy, really. It's called Blind Man's Buff.'

'Blind Man's Buff?' I say. 'I've played that at kid's parties – well, I think I have. I suppose we're talking about the same game?'

'More or less,' says Sylvia. 'Follow me through the rhododendrons. I have my own private glade. It's terribly bosky, don't you think?'

'Er–yes,' I say, watching the shrubbery close in around us. 'Tell me more about this game.'

'Well,' says Sylvia. 'It's terribly simple – and you might almost say childish. The whole purpose is to make the players come to terms with their bodies without embarrassment. We often use it when people are coming to the sanctuary for the first time.'

'Yes, but what happens?' I say, trying to keep the eagerness out of my voice.

'To many people, appearing naked in front of their fellow human beings for the first time is terribly embarrassing – you've experienced that yourself. As for actually touching! Well, that's quite beyond the compass of most people. They either suffer acute withdrawal symptoms or, sometimes, as in your case, go in quite the opposite direction.'

'Yes,' I say. 'I know what you mean.'

'By blindfolding people it's been found that you remove half the area of anxiety immediately. They can't see and therefore they're not embarrassed.'

'Except when they put their hand in the custard,' I say.

'Silly!' says Sylvia. 'They're not blindfolded all the time. Only when they're playing the game. Ah, here we are.'

Like she said we would, we have arrived in a small woodland glade surrounded by trees and shrubs. The grass is green and inviting and there is a circle of blue above our heads. Somewhere in the trees, pigeons are cooing. At moments like this I can see what Sid was getting at on Clapham Common.

'Very nice,' I say. 'Now, what happens when you're blindfolded?'

'The second phase of contact can begin without recrimination,' says Sylvia. 'It's jolly super.' She brushes a cheeky insect off one of her noble knockers and I nod – I wish it was only with my head.

'Because people can't see each other they don't feel threatened or embarrassed. They can touch without fear. Once they've got used to the sensation of naked flesh brushing – or buffing – against their own they can put the whole range of physical sensations in perspective. Do you understand?'

'So you – er touch each other, do you?' I ask. 'You don't have to stick anything—'

'No,' says Sylvia. 'That's the other game. We call this Blind Man's Buff because of the obvious connotations of buffing and because it makes it easier for people to begin to participate if they can persuade themselves that what is really encounter therapy is no more than a game.' She gives a nervous giggle. 'Perhaps I shouldn't be giving the game away. I don't want my explanation to inhibit you.

'You think this might – er help me, do you?' I say.

'I think it's worth a shot,' says Sylvia. 'We've got to do something with you. You could hurt yourself going about like that.'

There is what looks like a small first aid box nailed to a tree at the edge of the clearing and Sylvia opens it and removes a couple of furry eyepads. 'There was a robin's nest in there last year,' she says. 'It was absolutely super seeing their little mouths opening.'

I nod my agreement and have a crafty shufti at my mask. I won't fancy it overmuch if a nestful of robins have been having a tom tit over it. 'You're going to put one on as well, are you?' I ask.

'Oh yes,' says Sylvia. 'It's got to be the same for both of us. It wouldn't be proper Blind Man's Buff otherwise, would it?'

'No, of course not,' I say. 'Well – er when you're ready.' I gaze at the melting curve carnival and can hardly believe my luck. What a beautiful bird. Her body willows in and out like a slim violin and just to look at her makes percy feel like Beau Pummel. Her bristols carry more weight than any British delegate in the Common Market and stand out proudly from her body with the nipples quivering like the noses of eager pointers. And talking of eager

123

pointers – yes! If I walked towards her with my arms behind my back there would be no doubt about which bit of me would start buffing first.

'Ready?' She stands in front of me with her mask in her hands and you might say that I am quivering with anticipation.

'When I give the word, we'll both put our masks on and move towards each other. One, two, three. Go!'

I take a quick butchers round the glade to make sure that we are still on our tods and slip on my mask. The last thing I see is Sylvia's boobs giving a little jump as her germans go back to adjust the elastic round her flowing barnet and it is a very pleasant memory – or perhaps I should say mammary – to take into the world of darkness. Even though I can't see Sylvia I have a picture of her in my mind as clearly as if it had been projected against the inside of my nut. I step forward and stretch out a hand and – bingo! I don't need a lucky dipple to find her nipple. It is just where I thought it would be – like the light switch inside my bedroom. I don't want to appear too forward too soon so I leave go of the strawberry and slide my powerful arms round the coachwork. We meet in more places than an adulterous couple and when I brush against her fanny cranny I don't have to look at the nook to get the feeling that it's appealing.

'I'm sorry,' I say.

'Ssh,' she says. 'Talking's not allowed. Anyway, you needn't feel ashamed. This is what it's for – to get it all out of your system.' She returns the pressure of my arms and brushes one of her mits over my fife and down to the backs of my bridges. Phew! It is a good job I have ruthless self control or she might be getting something out of my system a bit sooner than she bargains for. I allow a shiver to run through my body – in fact I allow two because the first one enjoyed it so much – and slide my own hands

124

over her beautiful bot. It is like a firm peach and cuts into her thighs so sharply that my mit has to slow down before it runs out of curve. I turn my head sideways and brush my lips against her barnet, feeling the texture of the elastic that holds her mask in place. I pluck at it with my teeth and move my right hand into the cleft between her back buffers – blind man's buffers. I hear her suck in her breath and she gives a little gasp which coincides with my north and south making clumsy contact with her cakehole. I give her a tongue sandwich with a dressing of relish and brush my chest across her knockers. If contact is the name of the game then our performance cannot be faulted. I cool the pressure of my hands and let my lips, teeth and tongue do the talking. First on her mouth and then in the area of her upper body – her nipples must be the highest points for miles. 'Oooh!' A small sigh escapes her lips as my hooked forefinger tickles the entrance to her gravy boat and her own looks and lingers brush against my rampant hive bomber. I press forward so that my metric munificence lies upright against her curved belly and stretch out a long finger to explore the nearby spasm chasm. Uuhm. This lady is in much better condition for a spot of the other than half a sack of rusty wing nuts. I wonder how far you are allowed to go in Blind Man's Buff, Little Crumbling style? There seems only one way to find out. I move both hands to Sylvia's rocks and boulders and mould her to my lips like I have plans to corrugate them against my Teds. As the pressure builds up, so does her grip on my hampton as she responds to the passion of my hit or miss. Powerful forces are clearly at work and I see no reason why percy should not be one of them. Easing the joystick forward as far as its rampant condition will allow I make contact with the lubricated landing field nestling in the bush. My flight path is not an easy one and I bend my knees and prepare to make another run, this time reckoning on the up and under approach to achieve my objective. Alas, no sooner have my cobblers taxied along Sylvia's thighs and my nose cone penetrated her banger hangar than she disengages and takes a step backwards. Curses! Don't say I am only allowed to touch her outside?

'Come.' To my relief – or I hope it will be to my relief – Sylvia feels for my hand and draws me after her. 'I know a place.' Great! She is clearly leading me off for a spot of secret chaver. It could not happen to a nicer bloke. I like this game, I really do. I take a couple of steps and – 'Ouch!' My toe thumps into a root and I let go of Sylvia's hand and hop around a bit while I give it some massage, my toe, I mean. When I reckon it will still work I put it down and feel about me for Sylvia. Knickers! I can't find her.

'Sylvia?' I call out her name very softly. There is no answer but I hear a rustling to my right. The little temptress has clearly got some hiding place in the middle of a bush – apart from the one we all know about. Putting a protective mit round percy who is standing out like the icebreaker on a Russian trawler, I make careful progress in the direction of the rustling noise. It seems to have stopped now but that is probably because Sylvia is poised, limp and eager, for my coming. I am tempted to lift my eye pads and have a quick peep but that would be cheating and I don't want to spoil our game. Also, there is no doubt that it is sexy, stumbling and fumbling and feeling against the unknown. Especially in the open air. My hand makes contact with some leaves and I brush them to one side and advance carefully. I seem to be in another open space with soft, springy grass beneath my feet. I wonder—? Ah! My knee bumps against wood and almost immediately I feel female flesh. Oh, what delight. Sylvia is clearly stretched out on one of the rustic benches that litter the gardens. I would like to hold back but there comes a time when the call of nature is too strong. When a man must do what a man has to do. This delectable mother of pearl must be harpooned on my funny gun without further ado. Running my hand lightly up the inside of Sylvia's leg I dive it into her minge fringe and cast myself down on top of her. What enormous knockers she has when you find them up against your chest. What—

'YAAAAARGGGHHHH!!' The body beneath me rises up like a basking whale disturbed in mid-kip and my bum hits the ground split seconds later. The force of impact dislodges my eye pads and when I look up it is to see – oh no! – Mrs Lestrange staring down at me, her face a mixture of horror and rage.

CHAPTER SEVEN

In which Sid prepares to welcome C.U.N.T. and Rosie arrives.

'Bleeding marvellous!' says Sid. 'There am I on the point of finalising some highly sophisticated negotiations and you have to put everything in jeopardy by trying to rape the ugliest bleeding woman in the colony!'

'I wasn't trying to rape her!' I protest. 'I was playing Blind Man's Buff.'

'More like Blind Man's *Muff* from what I hear,' says Sid. 'Honestly, you do have some funny ways. I've heard of blokes being attracted to older women but this is ridiculous!'

'It was the mask,' I say. 'I couldn't—'

'Yeah that was pretty kinky,' interrupts Sid. 'I couldn't see why you did that. Was it because you couldn't stand the sight of her? Or was it so she had a chance to get away? Very sporting of you. I'm glad to see that British traditions still prevail even amongst rapists.'

'It's not like everybody thinks,' I say. 'You ought to ask Sylvia – if you can find her,' I might add. She and her Mum and Dad checked out of the sanctuary shortly after the unfortunate misunderstanding.

'Or maybe you didn't want her to recognise you,' muses Sid. 'Of course, a smart rapist would have made some holes in the mask so he could see out. You might think of that next time. It's little details like that can make all the difference between success and failure.' He looks at me closely and shakes his head. 'I worry about you sometimes.

I'm not surprised that Farmer Dropwort is disturbed about your relationship with his pig.

'She hasn't been around again, has she?' I ask.

'No, but he has,' says Sid. 'It's a good job he wears a hat otherwise I wouldn't have been able to tell the difference. They both use the same after shave lotion.'

'I'm certain it's nothing to worry about,' I say. 'How did you get on with Cherry?'

'Er – yes,' says Sid. 'Interesting girl. Very responsible. I think she could take a lot more weight on her shoulders.'

'I hadn't approached it like that,' I say. 'Still, I see what you mean.'

'I think she should be giving head – I mean-er, given her head!' says Sid blushing. 'I believe that you will find she comes into her own when we welcome C.U.N.T.'

The prospect is one to make the mind boggle and it takes me a few moments to speak. 'C.U.N.T.?' I say weakly.

'Confederation of United Nude Travellers,' says Sid. 'I'm arranging for them to hold a seminar here. It should really put the place on the map.'

'Commercial travellers?' I say. 'Blimey, they must have a difficult time. It's bad enough having to flog brushes without arriving on the doorstep in the buff. I can just imagine it. You ring the doorbell. "Good morning, madam, I'm selling brushes." "Right, I'll have that one." She grabs hold of your willy and you're a hospital case on your first call.'

'Have you taken leave of your senses?' scolds Sid. 'You really must learn to control that vivid imagination of yours and get a few more facts inside your noddle. C.U.N.T. is one of the most respected organs in world nudism. Its members travel round the globe spreading the massage – I mean, the message.'

'They're coming here?' I say. 'To Little Crumbling?'

'Yes,' says Sid proudly. 'The naked body will never have got so much coverage in this part of the world. I have already informed the Beet Growers' Gazette and the national newspapers. Reporters will soon be flocking in by every brewer's drey.'

'That's wonderful, Sid,' I say. 'If only we had some caravans on the site.'

'We will have,' says Sid. 'My mighty advertising campaign has already swung into action. Whilst you have been trying to thrust your blindfold nasty into Mrs Lestrange and narrowly avoiding proceedings being taken as well as umbrage, I have been getting down to it with Cherry. She speaks my language.'

'Even with her mouth full?' I venture. 'This is an astonishing gift.'

'Thank you on her behalf,' says Sid rubbing his hands together. 'Oh Timmo, I really believe I've cracked it this time. The simple pastoral idyll, plus a few bob in your pocket at the same time. I don't know why I never got into naturism before. The feeling of sun against your bare flesh. The sweet kiss of a barmy breeze. You know, I feel uncomfortable with clothes *on* these days.'

'Yes,' I say. 'It will be interesting to see how Rosie takes to it all.'

Sid's brow contracts like a deflating concertina. 'Rosie?' he says sharply.

'Yes. It will be interesting to see how she responds to life in the raw. You know, taking all her clothes off. I expect the kiddies will—'

'Taking all her clothes off?' says Sid, turning the colour of a Tanzanian's tummy. '*My wife!* Are you mad? I'm not having Rosie wandering about in the buff with everybody gawping at her! What a disgusting idea. I'd better ring her up and tell her not to come. It might upset the children.'

'You don't have to ring her up, Sid,' I say. 'Isn't that her getting out of that taxi at the gate?'

'What!' Sid spins round so fast that his crust nearly jumps off his shoulders. 'Oh no!' He starts striding towards the gate and I follow him.

When we get there, Rosie is standing with her hands on her hips, surveying the field as if it is unlikely to take the place of Tom Jones in her store of wish fulfilment.

'Hello, my darling,' says Sid. 'Didn't you see me waving at you? You shouldn't have let that taxi go.'

'Why? Are we expected to sleep in it?' says Rosie, bitterly. 'Put that toad down, Jason, You don't know where it's been – not down Jerome's neck! Ooh, I've had enough of you two to last me a lifetime!'

'I'm afraid there is a problem, dear heart,' says Sid. 'I'm arranging for some caravans to be permanently on the site but they haven't arrived yet. I'm sorry but I think it might be best if—'

'There's always the sanctuary, Sid,' I say. 'I mean, The Wonderful World of—'

'No!' Sid almost shouts the word. 'I mean, no. I couldn't expect Rosie and the kids to – er—'

'What are you talking about, Timmy?' says Rosie impatiently.

'I want to go to the seaside!' says Jason.

'I want to go to the toilet!' says Jerome.

'You can't do!' says Rosie. 'You went in the taxi.'

'It's a big house, nice gardens, Sid,' I say apologetically. 'They've got some spare rooms, we know that.'

'What are you two on about?' says Rosie. 'Don't say you've brought us all the way up here for nothing Sid, or I'll crown you!'

Sid looks desperate. 'It's the children I'm worried about,' he says.

'Since when?' snorts Rosie. 'It's me who always gets

lumbered with them. Stop doing that to your brother, Jason!'

'He started it, Mum!' yelps Jason. 'He hit me back.'

'I'll hit your back if you don't belt up!' snaps Sid, turning on the kid. 'You haven't acknowledged my existence yet. Haven't you got a word for your father?'

'Yes, but Mum won't let us use it,' says the child pirhana.

I step between him and his father hurriedly. 'Let's not get heated,' I say. 'This is something of a family reunion, really, isn't it?'

'Shut up!' says Sid. He rounds on Rosie. 'If you spent more time teaching the kids manners and less time poncing about in your boutiques and wine bars they might show a little respect for their father!'

'Listen, you big jerk!' says Rosie. 'I spend twice as much time with the kids as you do and if it wasn't for the money I bring in we wouldn't have the home we have now. In fact, we'd be better off if you stayed at home and I went out to work.'

'Mum's right,' says Jason who can always smell a good punch up.

'Anybody know the words of "Happy Days Are Here Again"?' I ask.

It is sad isn't it? I remember when Rosie would wash Sid's underpants like Michael York had blown his nose on them. Now, the magic has gone. The first bit of bees Sid ever made gave her the chance to open a boutique and she has never looked back. The whole of their trendy Vauxhall – or South Westminster as the new residents call it – pad was furnished by her with stuff that it is painful to sit on, look at or eat off and Sid looks more and more uncomfortable in his surroundings. That is probably why he spends so much time round at our house in Scraggs Lane where he and Rosie started married life. He belongs there with his lip curled up over one of Mum's diabolical cups of tea. Rosie has moved on. Sid has not.

'Oh look,' says Jason. 'There's a rude lady waving at Dad. I can see her titties.'

Sid glares at Jason like he would love to give him a giraffe woman neck without the aid of the metal rings and we all turn to see Cherry leaning through a gap in the hedge that surrounds the sanctuary – or 'W.W.O.N.' as Sid insists in calling it. Her knockers are indeed very noticeable.

'She must want her clothes back, Sidney,' says Rosie, in a voice that could cause storm cones to be hoisted. 'I hope I didn't arrive at an awkward moment?'

Sid swallows hard and raises his chin. 'Rosie, there's something I think you ought to know,' he says.

'I think I already know it,' says Rosie. She removes her shoulder bag and starts wrapping the strap round her wrist.

'No!' says Sid. 'You don't understand. Miss Balsam is under me.'

'I understand that,' says Rosie through pursed lips. 'I understand that perfectly!' She starts striding towards the hedge and I grab Sid's arm. I remember what she did to Millicent Honeywood when we were both kids – and she was only riding her tricycle.

'Stop her, Sid!' I yelp. Sid is standing there like a man watching his mother-in-law drive over a cliff in his new car and it takes a few moments before he jars into action.

'Rosie!' he barks. 'Come back here. What do you think—? Ouch!'

He says 'ouch!' in sympathy with Cherry who has just copped Rosie's handbag round the kisser.

'Do her, Mum!' says Jason loyally.

'Waaaaaah!!' wails Jerome.

The two women collapse through the hedge struggling

133

viciously and Sid plunges after them. I sweep up Jason and Jerome and bear their reluctant bodies towards the beach. 'Come on!' I say, trying to inject a note of cheer. 'Uncle Timmy will show you where the land mines used to be!'

CHAPTER EIGHT

In which Timmy is forced to go to unusual lengths in order to find a suitable candidate for The Miss Nude World contest.

'There you are,' says Sid. 'That's more like it, isn't it? It just took a bit of time, that's all. Cromer wasn't built in a day, you know.'

We are standing, naked, of course, inside the grounds of the Wonderful World of Nudism – oops! Sorry: W.W.O.N. – and peering through the bright green leaves at the site of Noggett Super Hols. It is two weeks after the initial unpleasantness between Rosie and Cherry – Cherry's black eye has nearly disappeared – and Sid has got used – well, almost used – to his wife and kids frisking around in the nude. Jason has practically stopped saying 'he's got a big one, Mum!' and everybody has high hopes that Jerome will learn to stop playing with himself – especially during meals. It is a topic that sparks off a lot of conversation about the right age at which to start taking your children on a nudist holiday. Whatever their differences, most people agree that the kids must be older than Jason and Jerome.

'Yes, Sid,' I say. 'I never thought I'd live to see people actually bringing their caravans here. It just shows the power of advertising.'

'The smoke from the beet processing plant is holding off well, too,' says Sid. 'It's never a problem when it keeps above ground level.'

'Exactly,' I say. 'And you can hardly niff the sewage works – except when there's a squall. If it wasn't for the drizzle everything would be perfect.'

'They look happy enough,' agrees Sid. 'And the Day Admittance queue is building up nicely. Come on, my beauties! Let's have you!'

Sid is referring to the shuffling line of middle-aged men in plastic macs and stained pork pie hats that is stretching away from the corrugated iron pay box built between the W.W.O.N. and the caravan site. Cherry takes their money and they pass into one of Sid's horse boxes to remove their clothes and enter The Wonderful World of Nudism for two and a half hours of unrelieved goggling – though there is some doubt as to how unrelieved it is after disturbing accounts of what has taken place behind the bushes. Mr Friar is most upset about it, but Sid tells him that it is perfectly normal and does not affect your sight, and anyhow, they have handed over their money before they enter the grounds.

The one thing I am not convinced about is Sid's plan to convert the horse boxes into rentable caravans. Even the one's with room for two horses are not very big – and even smaller when they still have the horses in them. Even Sid was surprised at that – I mean, that they still had the horses in them. He says that there must have been some misunderstanding even though they are very old horses – very old horses with virtually no control over their Enochs. It does show as you try and pick your way down to the beach – which fewer and fewer people are tending to do since the Liberian tanker sprang a leak and an oil slick clogged the sand up to the cliffs. 'Black pool,' is what some wag called the place, after the incident

At the same time I do think that the warning signs about the cliff falls, the quicksands and the dangerous currents have had a discouraging effect on our customers – though Sid has acted positively and done what seemed right to him in the circumstances, eg tried to tear out all the warning signs. Fortunately, perhaps, the Council has sunk them in concrete and this is impossible.

'When are they due?' I say.

'Any minute now,' says Sid glancing at the spot on his wrist where his watch would be if he was not stark, bollock naked. 'The coach was supposed to pick them up from the airport early this morning.'

'I still think we should have put a bit of punctuation in that sign,' I say. 'I mean, C-U-N-T without any stops is asking for trouble, isn't it?'

'I always pull the stops out when I see a bit of C-U-N-T!' says Sid, slapping me on the shoulder. 'Get it? I do! Ha, ha.'

I let the last, coarse guffaw escape from his body and relieve myself of a deep sigh. This boy is not going to cause Peter Lawford any sleepless nights.

'I had a great idea which I didn't tell you about,' says Sid, impervious to my lack of enthusiasm for his diabolical pleasantry. 'The press are going to lap it up.'

'Yes, whatever happened to them?' I ask. 'Even the geezer from the Beet Growers' Gazette never got in touch. You'd think that anybody associated with making sugar would be glad of a scoop.' I wait for some acknowledgement of my scintillating shaft of wit, but not a sausage. Sometimes I think I have outgrown Sid.

'They'll need their heads examined if they miss out on this lot,' says Sid with satisfaction. 'The first Miss Nude World contest ever held at Little Crumbling!'

'A beauty contest?' I say.

'Something much more than that,' says Sid. 'When you think of beauty contests you think of Eric Morley and Michael Aspel and I prefer birds myself. I want to get back to the natural loveliness of the unadorned female body. I see it more as a ceremony. An expression of purity and hope. A return to simple values in a world of crass commercialism – which reminds me, we treble the day admittance charges when the contest is on.'

'That's a bit steep, isn't it?' I say.

'It'll help to keep the undesirable element out,' says Sid. 'Or conversely, it will serve them right for being undesirable – look what's this? It must be them!'

What appears to be a convoy of hooting cars and ton-up boys is approaching past the caravan site, led by a coach. Yes, there is no doubt that it is them. I can see the large CUNT sign from here. Oh dear, I do wish Sid had taken my advice about the punctuation. He is now hurrying up the drive towards the gate and I lengthen my stride after him.

The gatekeeper, now – on Sid's instructions – wearing a loin cloth – it looks blooming silly with his hobnailed boots and peaked cap – is wrestling with the wire gate and trying to let the coach in and keep the surging multitude out. Prominent amongst them I recognise Walter Looney, the front of his smock covered with cuckoo spit – or maybe it is saliva.

'Blimey, Sid!' I say. 'I didn't know they were going to come starkers!'

'No,' says Sid. 'It does look a bit strange, doesn't it? Fifty naked birds in coach marked CUNT. No wonder they've got the police escort.'

'And all the other ones,' I say. 'Please! Get back! Shove off! Get out of it!' The atmosphere around the gate is heated and it is with relief that the gatekeeper eventually slams the gate against the mob – short-lived relief because he finds that his loin cloth is still snagged to it.

'I think we'd better greet them at the house,' says Sid. 'I was going to say a few words but—' he breaks off as his eyes sweep over the crowd milling round the gates and he takes a pace forward. 'Admittance through the caravan site. Please try and have the right change handy. Fuzz half price.' He runs out of breath and steps back. 'Stupid to miss an opportunity,' he says.

'Sid,' I say. 'Did you get a decco at those birds? There wasn't a looker amongst them. And there were quite a lot of blokes.'

'That's no problem,' says Sid. 'We'll have a Mr Nude Universe title as well. That way we'll get twice the exposure. Don't worry about the birds. There must be one or two of them that are all right.'

Half an hour later, Sid is not so sure. 'That North Korean bird isn't bad,' he says. 'She's got pretty hair.'

'Yeah, but the colour clashes with her moustache,' I say. 'Honestly, Sid. If you took the best feature from all of them you'd end up with a duff version of Hattie Jacques.'

Sid looks thoughtful. 'I wonder if she'd do it?' he says. 'Why don't you ring up her agent? Maybe—'

'Don't be daft, Sid!' I say. 'She's not going to save us. There's only one thing for it: you'll have to cancel the contest.'

'It's too late,' says Sid. 'I've had a number of acceptances from the press already. The loss of face would be too great.'

'You could certainly do with losing some of the faces around here,' I say. 'I keep waiting for them to take off their masks.'

'We'll have to find some new blood,' says Sid. 'I wonder if any of the ladies on the caravan site – wait a minute! I've got an idea. That Dimity bird was a bit of all right. She'd look very fair in the papers. We could lose the others in the background. Get round there and chat her up. I'd go myself but you know what it's like with Rosie. She's so infatuated with me that she might get the wrong idea.'

'What am I going to say, Sid?' I ask. 'I can't just come straight out with it.'

'You'll have to lead up to it,' says Sid. 'Start giving her one and then tell her how lovely she looks in the buff. Be subtle. It always works with me.'

'Thanks a lot,' I say. 'You want to put that in a book. You could have Barbara Cartland on the dole.'

'Stop rabbiting and get round there,' says Sid. 'I'll have a word with Cherry. She might go in for it.' He looks round and shakes his head. 'If only some of them could speak English. Look at that bird over there eating the daffodils! It gets you down after a while.'

'Don't worry,' I say. 'Rosie is trying to explain to her. She has settled in well, hasn't she?'

Sid does not say anything but grinds his Teds together and I know I have touched on a delicate subject – like playing chicken with your old man and a live rail. Rosie has taken to the nudist life like a duck to LSD and Sid is not really happy at the thought of other blokes having a butchers at her vital statistics. He keeps trying to get her to go home but Rosie says she likes the life and is staying – and when Rosie says something, that's it. No arguments.

I leave Sid making arrangements for the press conference – eg watering down the gin so they don't pass out before anything has been said – and slide down to the gatehouse where I slip into my threads. There are still a few sightseers outside the gate but I push my way through them saying, 'No comment, no comment,' like the union leaders do when they leave 10 Downing Street carrying Harold's shirt and trousers, and stride purposefully towards the Dropwort abode. I am well aware that I am not a star attraction as far as Dan is concerned and it is while I am pondering my best method of approach to Bitter Vetch Farm that I hear the sound of a tractor behind me. I turn and – what a turn up – or perhaps I should say, what a turnip! There is Dimity driving the tractor which is pulling a trailer load of beet.

'Dimity!' I sing out. 'What a fantastic coincidence! I was just coming round to see you. You're looking great!'

She is wearing what must be her Dad's army greatcoat, a head scarf and bright yellow Wellington boots so you can see I am laying it on a bit.

'You be just saying that,' she says, idling her engine. 'I bet you tell that to all the girls that be taking their crop to the beet processing plant.'

'Not a beet of it – I mean, bit of it,' I say. 'I'm absolutely serious. I've missed you terribly since we left the farm. I've thought about you a lot.'

Dimity fiddles coyly with the split in one of her motor cycle gauntlets. 'I don't know that I can believe 'ee,' she says. 'I reckon that you loves my da's pig more than me.'

'That's rubbish!' I say. 'The relationship between me and Mabel has been blown up out of all proportion. It was you I was looking for that night.'

'If only I could believe 'ee,' says Dimity. 'I was drawn to 'ee 'tis true but when I came in search of my heart's desire, 'twas the other gen'leman planted his mangle wurzel.'

'Don't remind me,' I say with a shudder. 'It nearly broke my heart. Oh, how different our lives might have been if I had turned right at the ferrets.'

Whilst we are both considering this romantic possibility, a Rover 3500 with a 'PRESS' sticker on the windscreen hoots to a halt behind the tractor and reminds me that there is no time to lose. I need to achieve a whirlwind wooing if the Miss Nude World contest is going to be saved from disaster.

'I'll pull over,' says Dimity.

'Don't bother,' I say. 'I'll hop on the back. I'll follow you to the beet processing plant – or the end of the world. Whichever is nearer!'

Who says romance is dead? You can tell from the look

in her eyes that my words have touched her – and if my words, why not the rest of me? Make no mistake, lads, a few pretty phrases go a long way with the ladies and if you have my mind-boggling facility, you're a mug if you don't use it. Holding her glance for maximum effect, I vault lightly over the side of the trailer and nearly remove my cluster on one of the metal uprights. The love light dies in my eyes and is replaced by a look that must be pretty close to agony. There is a muffled guffaw from the Rover and it overtakes in a cloud of Vat 69 fumes. Bloody reporters!

'Be you all right?' inquires Dimity solicitously. 'Keep your eye open for a dock leaf. That be a powerful balm.'

I thank her for her interest and sink down amongst the sugar beet. It is not over comfortable but at least I can rearrange it so that there is a dip in the middle with a barricade of beet all round it. By the time we turn into the beet processing plant I can only see the top of the gate-posts.

'Pull on to the grass!' I say urgently. 'I want to talk to you.'

'What are you doing up there?' says Dimity coyly.

'Come up and find out!' I husk. 'I've got a surprise for you. There's something here I'd like your opinion on.'

'Bet it ain't no sugar beet!' says Dimity, getting my drift swiftly. 'Hang on a minute. I'll park against the delivery bay. They must be having their tea break at the moment.' There is an encouraging strain of interest in her voice and I allow myself a flicker of hope and a twinkle of the winkle. Maybe I can pull it off.

Dimity reverses the trailer against the factory and I pray that nothing will arise to interrupt our idyll. The next few moments are crucial. 'Now, what be 'ee a doing of?' Dimity's head appears over the tail board and I stretch out my arms imploringly.

'Come here!' I gasp. 'Lie with me.' A bit of passion always goes down a treat with the birds, even if you are lying on a pile of sugar beet, and I can see that Dimity is drawn.

'Do I ought to?' she says. 'Do I really ought to? What would my da' say? And you walking out with his pig.'

'Forget Mabel!' I hiss. 'She means nothing to me. The feeling is all on her side. It's you I yearn for, churn for and burn for!'

Shakespeare might have put it differently but he could not have improved on the response. Hardly pausing to look round, Dimity has her gumboot over the side of the trailer and is soon snuggling down beside me in a small avalanche of sugar beet.

'What did 'ee want to show me – I hope?' she says, playfully stroking my nose with an errant mangle wurzel.

'Well,' I say. 'I don't know how to put it but—'

'I do!' says Dimity eagerly. 'There be no need to be shy. Living on a farm one gets to know about these things. One sees the bulls and the chickens – not together, of course.'

'Of course,' I say. 'Yes, so—'

'Don't 'ee worry 'eself,' says the wench encouragingly. 'Dimity'll dandle yor handle.'

She is as good as her word and dives her mit into the beet like it is the surface of a bran tub. Our lips collide and her country fresh knockers thrust me backwards. 'You're beautiful,' I gasp, forcing myself to come to grips with the purpose of the exercise. 'You have a lovely body.'

'Thankee,' she says. 'I'd like to show it to you but it be a bit parky up here, bain't it? Best if I just wriggle out of my nicks. It's moments like this that I envy youm fellows.'

I see what she means when she lies back and tries to pull her panties over her Wellington boots. She is half buried in beet before we eventually get them off – both Wellies and knicks.

'You have fantastic legs,' I breathe. 'Have you ever thought of modelling?'

'My da' bought me one of them Airfix kits,' she says. 'But I never really took to it. I prefer watching the radio.'

Truly an unspoilt child of nature, I think to myself – stupid, too. Still, she is definitely a looker and when she takes off her head scarf and her golden tresses flop all over the beet it is no hardship for my cock to imagine that it has fallen a little in love with her.

'Look,' I husk, spilling kisses on to her soft, warm lips. 'With a body like yours you could be famous. Take my advice. Enter for the Miss Nude World contest. I know you could win it – in fact, I can guarantee that you could win it. It could be the first step to Mecca!'

'What be I want to walk to the Middle East for?' she says glancing at the beet stacked around us. 'My roots be here.'

Whilst I am thinking about this and wondering if Sid will understand the problem I am having, Dimity sensually starts to undo the buttons of her great coat and reveal that she is wearing a mini-skirted dress beneath it. She writhes deeper into the beet and furls her lips temptingly.

'Come 'ee here!' she husks. 'Let's have a sight o' yor wurgler!' She does not wait for a reply but returns her hand to the root of so many of my problems and proceeds to pull open my fly with the delicacy of a mechanical grab being operated on a piecework basis. Her skirt has ridden up her thighs and a flash of pubes is all that is required to ignite my lurking loin lizard. Percy comes to hand like a stick of rock that needs no message through the middle and Dimity runs her hand up and down his length and opens her legs invitingly.

'Put him in!' she breathes. 'I be ready for a bit of crop rotation.'

She wriggles her hips enticingly and percy heads for her grumble like he has slipped a leash. As is always the way, the rest of my body has to follow him and I scramble over the sugar beet on hands and knees. 'Come on!' An expression akin to strain has appeared on Dimity's face and it is clear that she is looking forward to her encounter with the narrow marrow arrow. At last, I find some kind of kneehold on the shifting mass of beet between her thighs and position myself before the entrance to her snatch. This is it. The moment of ecstasy is nye. Both our expressions say it. Unable to restrain herself, Dimity grabs between my legs and thrusts deep and hard into her fanny cranny. Immediately, her face lights up and her mouth jumps open in spontaneous pleasure.

'Aaaah!' she gasps. 'That be heaven!'

'Ah hem!' I say. 'I'm sorry but I think you've got one of the sugar beet.'

It is terribly embarrassing, isn't it? Perhaps I should have lain there and said nothing but she must have realised after a bit, mustn't she – I mean, mustn't she? I do hope so. As it is I can't help feeling deflated. There is no point in pretending that our relationship is ever going to be quite the same after this. Whatever happens, I will always have the shadow of that beet hanging over me.

'Silly me,' says Dimity, swiftly rectifying her mistake. 'Ah, that be it, bain't it? There be no comparison, really.'

I am not totally comforted by this remark and it is with difficulty that I keep my giggle stick to the straight and not very narrow. I don't like to be unkind, but Dimity is a bit like those fridges that you see advertised as slim on the outside and big on the inside. My peace of mind is not improved by the sound of hangar doors sliding back and a man's voice saying: 'Right, gals! 'Ere be the next lot for the sorting line.'

Before I can disengage myself from Dimity Dropwort and the sugar beet that is pressing in all around me, I hear the tailboard drop and feel myself falling backwards as if tumbling down a steep incline. A line of rollers make contact with my action man kit – for action read inertia – and I find myself bumping along a conveyor belt surrounded by screeching women. They are all wearing turbans but somehow I don't think I have arrived at the sultan's harem.

CHAPTER NINE

In which Timmy gets to grips with the press in order to save The Wonderful World of Nudism.

'Where have you been?' asks Sid.

'Would you believe, being graded in the beet processing plant?'

'Don't mess about!' says Sid.

'That's what I told them,' I say. 'Oh, Sid. I can't begin to tell you what it was like—'

'Good,' says Sid. 'Because there isn't time. Where's Dimity?'

'I couldn't get her to come,' I say. 'Actually, it's a long story. You see, we got separated on the—'

'Blimey!' says Sid, burying his face in his hands. 'That's all I need. I'll have to fall back on Cherry.'

'Again?' I say.

'Belt up!' says Sid. 'Take your clothes off and get on stage with the rest of them.'

'What!'

'I'm bringing the Mr Nude Universe contest forward. It'll give me time to try and find some bird who couldn't be arrested for assault with a deadly weapon by smiling at you.' Sid groans. 'At the moment, Miss Bulgaria is ahead in the betting and that's only because she's had her beard permed.'

'You can't be serious, Sid!' I say, peering through the curtain at the rows of crowded seats. 'The crackle of plastic macs alone could perforate your eardrums. Some of the reporters are still awake!'

'Courage!' says Sid, grasping my arm. 'These are desperate times. I'm looking to you for a five star performance out there. Try and perform with dignity and remember how much is at stake. Not only are you representing the Wonderful World of Nudism, but your country! – and that against a load of dagos, most of whom are poufdahs to boot!'

'Now you tell me,' I say. 'Thanks a bundle, Sid. Who's judging this thing?'

'A panel of columists,' says Sid, triumphantly. 'Dead cunning, eh? If they're personally involved they're certain to mention it, aren't they? Just so they can see their own names in print. Now, get your clothes off and give your pectorals the once over with the Johnson's Baby Oil. One slosh per competitor, that's the rule.'

I must still be dizzy from the pummelling of a ton of sugar beet and the fumbling of half a gross of female digits because I find myself stripping off my clobber and stumbling out on to the stage with what must be the rest of the competitors. A glance around me soon shows what I am up against – perish the thought. The crew of the good ship Fairy could muster a more impressive array of masculine muscle. I avoid a couple of playful jostles and am relieved to find myself standing next to a face I know.

'Hello, Mr Friar,' I say. 'This is a bit of a carry on, isn't it?'

'I have the very gravest doubts about the efficacy of the whole procedure,' shudders Friar. 'If I had known that the sanctuary was going to become a peep show I would never have—'

He breaks off as the curtain parts and some of the competitors around us make half-hearted attempts to strike muscular poses.

I search the audience for familiar faces and am relieved to find that there is nobody I recognise. Rosie clearly has more sense than to expose Jason and Jerome to this kind of thing. Let us hope that they are all down on the beach looking for stingrays. I grip my hands above my head and lunge forward in a pose borrowed from one of the small ads in the comics I used to read when I was a kid: 'Let me make a man of you!' 'Builds power-packed muscle in only seconds a day!'

There is a bird down in the front row with her hair pulled back from her face and she is not unfanciable. Severe but cool and aloof – the kind you want to humiliate and bend to your inexorable will. I catch her eye and she starts licking the end of her pencil. Oh dear, I wish she had not done that. I immediately suffer a nasty switch in the hampton and I know what that can lead to. I try and look elsewhere but it is no good. My mince pies are drawn back as surely as crack Italian troops fearing that thick fog will obscure their white flags. The bird now has the tip of her pencil in her mouth. Control, Lea! Stiff upper lip and limp hampton. No good! There is a shrill blast on a whistle and I am ordered off.

'Bloody marvellous!' groans Sid. 'You've got less control than a Football League referee at a Sunday School five-a-side tournament. You realise you could have won that, don't you? You had the whole thing nestling in the palm of your hand and you had to blow it. Talk about up shit creek. Now we're really in schtuck.'

'It was that bird in the front row,' I say. 'She was goading me.'

'Don't be daft!' says Sid. 'She was from "The Gentlewoman". It says so on her press card. You're the ruination of all my dreams, you really are. I was pinning all my hopes on you lending a touch of class to what must be the nearest I have ever come to an error of judgement – look at that Persian geezer! What does he think he's doing? And in front of everybody, too. Oh my Gawd.'

'I don't think Friar is very happy either,' I say.

'I don't blame him, where he's standing,' says Sid. 'That Dutch bloke was always a bit dodgy if you ask me. Sucking those little pink sweets with the nasty niff. I don't think I can stand much more.'

'Oh well,' I say. 'There's only the Miss Nude World contest and then it's all over.'

'With the accent on *all*,' says Sid. 'Oh dear, I don't think I'm going to be able to watch. It's going to be like a traction engine rally without the grace.'

I hate to see Sid when he is in a mood like this so the best thing to do is go somewhere where I don't have to look at him. It is with this end in view – plus all the other ends that are dangling about – that I prepare to step from the side of the dais and take a turn round the gardens. A last turn as it might well be. I cannot see Friar pushing ahead with the merger after this little lot. We will be forced back on screwing whatever money we can out of the caravan site. What a shame the shit-house has just fallen down.

'Excuse me.' I look up and it is the bird with the pencil from the front row. 'I'm Imogen Coghan. Press.' She says 'Press' like it is an instruction and when I look at her body I wish it was. Slim as England's chances in the next World Cup but with a couple of cracking top bollocks and legs right up to the armpit. She is wearing clothes, too, and that is a tremendous turn on. You have no idea what it is like when you are surrounded by naked middle-aged crumpet all day – especially when it has the marks of wicker work chairs all over the bums.

'Oh yes, Timmy Lea,' I say. 'Got everything you need, have you?'

'I'd love an interview.' Imogen's eyes flicker down to my action man kit. 'Is there anywhere we could be alone?' It may be my imagination but she seems to nod over my shoulder towards one of the first floor bedrooms behind me.

'Well – er,' I say, glancing round the gardens and then turning to look at the house. 'I suppose it's pretty empty inside at the moment.'

'Capital.' Imogen is already striding purposefully towards the side entrance. 'I'd like to try to get a personal view.'

'Oh, really?'

'Yes. Why you became a nudist. What you do when you're not nude. Upstairs?'

'What? Oh, yes. Fine.' I follow her up the stairs and we have to press against the wall – *really* press – as some of the Miss Nude World contestants ease themselves past.

'Big girls,' says Imogen.

'Very,' I say.

'I thought you had a good chance,' says Imogen shooting another crafty glance at my cluster. 'It was a pity about your – er accident.'

'These things happen,' I say, very casual-like. 'The body can be a capricious instrument' – impressive stuff, eh? I got that out of a story in 'Woman's Own'.

'How fascinating,' says Imogen. 'I can't wait to hear more. Will in here be all right?' Before I can answer she has swung open a door revealing a large double bedroom looking out on to the garden. Appropriately enough, there is a large double bed in it. Imogen sprawls across it and quickly brings her pencil to her lips. A pad appears in her hand. 'Now,' she says, waving her arm towards the bed as if it is the first thing that meets her eye. 'Make yourself comfortable and let's get down to it.'

'Er – right,' I say. 'What would you like to know?' The sound of applause and chatter drifting through the open window reminds me of my responsibility to Sid and W.W.O.N. If I can give this bird a nice bit for her magazine then it may be the one bright spot to show for the whole day.

'First of all,' she says, turning all husky and leaning towards me as I edge on to the bed. 'Tell me what nudism means to you. Why do you want to take all your clothes off and expose your body to me?'

'Well,' I say. 'Er – it's not you in particular – I mean, don't get me wrong. I've nothing against you. I'd be very happy to expose my body to you – well, I am at the moment, aren't I? What I mean is – would you mind repeating the question?'

Imogen's bosom heaves and she puts down her pad. 'You're flustered, aren't you? Is it because I'm wearing clothes?'

'Not particularly,' I gulp. 'I've seen birds in clothes before.'

'Perhaps it would be fairer if I took them off.'

'No,' I say. 'There's no need to – oh blimey!' Before I can ring up the Samaritans, she has plucked open the front of her blouse and shrugged off her jacket. Her bristols swing forward like drinking horns at a Viking banquet and I begin to get the drift of what is on her mind. I reckon that the column inches she is interested in are not the type normally associated with newspapers. In the ordinary course of things – or perhaps I should say coarse of things – I would not stand in her way if she demanded a bit of the other, but it seems incumbent upon me to remind her of her responsibilities to the organ which she serves – as opposed to the organ which is serving her – ho, ho. Oh well, please yourselves.

'Yes,' I say. 'Yes. I'm glad you asked me that question. Nudity has always been a part of my life ever since I was a baby. In fact, I was born without any clothes on. It seemed daring at the time but peoples attitudes change and—'

'I loved it when your thing started to go up,' she says. I watch her hand like it is a snake gliding towards my crutch. 'Do you think it would do it again?'

'No,' I say. 'Definitely not. Absolutely no chance. I can guarantee that—'

I break off as percy soars ceilingwards at the first touch of her hooked forefinger. 'What else would you like to know?' I slide off the bed like someone has set light to it and look desperately towards the door. Before I can take a step toward safety she has sped past me, turned the key in the lock and tossed it out of the window – the key, not the lock.

'What did you do that for?' I say.

'We don't want to be disturbed,' purrs Imogen. 'I've hardly got anything out of you yet.'

I cross to the window and look out. Thank God! The key is lying on a striped awning that curves down over the dais. Another ripple of applause rises to remind me of my responsibilities.

'Then there's the fresh air and the sun,' I say. 'Playing against your naked body. It's very hygienic. I mean, animals don't wear clothes – except my aunty's dachshund. And you can see that he doesn't like it. He's always rubbing his jacket against the lamp posts and' – I am forced to break off again when Imogen hooks her arm round my neck and forces most of her brewer's bung into my cake-hole. 'Look!' I gasp, breaking free with difficulty 'I hope you're going to get some of this down.'

'This is what I'm going to get down!' She unzips her skirt and pulls her panties and tights down to her knees in one movement. Before I can say 'eek!' she is standing before me naked except for a whiff of posh perfume. 'That's better,' she breathes. 'Now we meet on equal terms.'

'Yes,' I say. 'Very nice. You have achieved your purpose. I feel much more relaxed. Now, pick up your pencil and pad and I'll give you an exclusive statement.'

'Why don't you give me six inches of steaming cock?'

Blimey. It isn't half hard to get through to this woman. She doesn't seem to be exactly wedded to her craft. Some men might weaken but not Timothy Lea. Once I have made a decision on a matter of principle I am adamant. I am going to do my level best for Sid in his moment of need – correction, I am going to do my vertical best for Sid in his moment of need.

'It's no good carrying on like that,' I say. 'Get off your knees this minute! You ought to be ashamed of yourself – ooh! What would they say at The Gentlewoman—? – OH! Stop doing that and cop my statement: "A pure mind in a healthy body is—" Oooh! Aaaah! Eeeeh!!—'

It is no good. I can't go on. This woman is a disgrace to her profession and I will have to withdraw from her presence before I run the risk of causing Sid further embarrassment. I don't know whose bedroom we are in but they might return at any minute. Easily as I could succumb – or vice versa from the look of it – this is one occasion on which I will summon up all my resources of self control and – 'OOOOOOOH!'

With a superhuman effort I wrestle my nibbled nunga from the naughty lady and flee to the window. If I stretch out far enough I will just be able to reach – 'YEEEEE-AAAAARRRRGGGHHH!'

I don't know if Imogen means to do it but there is a saying about bewaring the fury of a woman scorned. Perhaps it was just a playful lunge. Anyhow, one minute I am stretching out of the window with my fingers brushing the key, the next, a powerful squidge of the orchestras has jolted me forward and I am rolling down the awning like heavy rain. Coincident with a burst of applause from the audience and a startled scream from myself, there is a

154

loud ripping noise and I hurtle through the air to land on something large and soft – I later discover it is Miss Nude Ghana, or rather, her knockers. I stop bouncing and look up half stunned to see a sight that makes me believe that I must be experiencing some kind of hallucinatory concussion. It is Rosie as I can never remember seeing her before. Rosie with a garland round her Gregory Peck. Rosie, stark bollockless naked.

CHAPTER TEN

In which Timmy and Sid move on and there is a more or less happy ending.

The next morning I am looking at the same sight. Only this time, on the cover of the *Daily Moon*. There is a photo of a very nude Rosie under the headline: 'Nudist Supremo Keeps Beauty Title In The Family'. Sid and I are having a late breakfast and my brother-in-law's eyes glitter like freshly polished gold pieces.

' "Nudist Supremo",' he says. 'That's quite nice really, isn't it?'

'That's you, is it?' I say. 'Yes Sid. Makes you seem a bit like Hitler but I suppose, when you come to think of it—'

'Unbelievable publicity,' beams Sid. 'The *Guardian*'s got it on the arts page. Cherry says the phone hasn't stopped ringing since eight o'clock this morning. There's a queue of caravans stretching back to the other side of the village.'

'But Rosie!' I say. 'Well, I never. Who'd have thought it. I knew she enjoyed the life but—'

'She did it for me,' says Sid defensively. 'Nothing else would have persuaded her to.'

'You asked her did you, Sid?'

Sid shakes his head violently. 'Oh no. It wasn't necessary. I would never have done it anyway. It was her own decision entirely – but for me. Know what I mean? I think it's amazing how she manages to look if she's actually enjoying it. Did you notice that?'

'I did actually,' I say. 'You'd never know the whole

thing was an asthma to her just by looking at that, would you?'

'You wouldn't,' says Sid. I help myself to another cup of tea and Sid looks out of the window towards the cliffs. 'Where is she?' I ask.

'Who, Rosie?' says Sid. 'Oh, she went back to London early with the kids. They all sent their love. Jerome said he was sorry about your leather jacket.'

'What else would you use to sharpen a razor blade?' I say. 'She went off a bit early, didn't she?'

'I think there were some TV and radio interviews lined up,' says Sid. 'It seemed sensible to get as much publicity as we could. We talked about it and I told her to go ahead.'

'Yes,' I say. Poor old Sid. Reading between the lines I can see the way his mind is working. Mrs Noggett embarking on another world shattering career as an international nudist. I wonder what Mum and Dad will think?

These and other thoughts are bombarding my nut when the door bursts open and a familiar face, plus supporting parts, pushes past a spluttering Mr Friar. 'All right, fock Jock! You can push off now.' The familiar harsh tones belong to the unlovable Pigerty, his beard bristling.

'That's no way to talk to Mr Nude Universe,' says Sid. 'It's lucky that you breathed on his glasses or he might have ripped you apart. Now, what can I do for you?'

'What can I do for you?' imitates Pigerty in a mocking voice. 'Well, my pratties. You can piss off out of it, that's what you can do for me!'

'What are you on about!?' I say, feeling the fires of agro stir in my veins. 'You can't tell us what to do.'

'Oh yes I can,' says Pigerty. 'You thought you were smart didn't you? Moving in with all your caravan sites and your nudist colonies. Well, I've got news for you. That paper you signed wasn't worth nothing! I still own the field. So thanks for setting up a nice little business for me and sling your hook!'

'It must be mine if you accepted money for it,' says Sid.

Pigerty dives his hand into his pocket and shoves a roll of dirty notes into Sid's face. 'Here's your money – plus a bit of interest for the work you've done. Now, do yourselves a favour and push off before I set the family on you!'

'Now you listen!' I say, giving him 'my mighty meatey, matey,' look. 'If you think—'

To my surprise, Sidney holds up a restraining hand and takes the money. 'Timothy, please! Let there be no unpleasantness. Remember the first rule of nudism: "He who turns the other cheek probably likes it in Wellington boots as well." If Mr Pigerty has changed his mind it is not for us to argue.'

'But Sid!' I say. 'For once we really look like cleaning up. Surely you're not going to be given the bum's rush by this—'

'Timothy, I have spoken.' Sid moves towards the door and beckons me after him urgently. 'Good luck and all the breast, Mr Pigerty.'

'Sid!' I say as we hurry down the drive. 'Are you trying for the Italian Victorian Cross? I've never known you run so fast. Surely you're not really scared of that big slob?'

'Get your clothes on and let's get out of here,' says Sid. 'I reckon we've got about four minutes.'

Three and a half minutes later I am walking towards the Rover which Sid is revving up outside the caravan site.

'I still don't see what all the hurry is about,' I say getting into the car. 'I reckon it was worth going to law.'

'I don't,' says Sid nodding towards the cliff edge. 'Do you see the car park?'

'No,' I say.

Sid eases his foot off the clutch. 'Neither do I. That's the trouble. I was looking out of the window when it disappeared. Just as that Pigerty geezer came into the kitchen. I was deciding between the Jag and the Jensen when "bam!" they weren't there any more.'

'Over the cliff!' I say.

'With the other thirty odd jam jars,' says Sid, opening the throttle. 'That must be the owners marching towards Friar's place.'

'Where they'll find Pigerty!' I say.

'Who of course owns the joint,' says Sid happily. 'He ought to do something about those cliff falls.' He taps the roll of notes in his top pocket. 'It hasn't worked out too badly, really. Rosie will be disappointed but you can't have everything.' He gives a relieved laugh and glances in the mirror. 'Blimey! Is that a pig running along behind us?'

I turn round. 'It's Mabel!'

'Ah well,' says Sid. 'It's nice to know that someone still fancies you.' He puts his foot down and Mabel veers off to the left and sits panting on the steps of the Three Jolly Rapists beside Walter Looney.

'She'll get over it,' says Sid. 'Time and booze are great healers.'